Fear gripped her as she inched forward

Then she stood trembling outside the door in the underground passage. The strip of light from under the door was all that pierced the pitch-blackness that surrounded her.

There was no sound but she knew someone was in there! Her pulse pounding in her ears, she opened the heavy latched door. The sudden brightness blinded her. When her eyes focused, she gasped. She had never expected the man she saw before her.

He smiled silkily. "I've been waiting for you, my dear."

Other

MYSTIQUE BOOKS
by LEO DARTEY

46 A STRANGER THREATENS
50 MIDNIGHT VISITOR

For a free catalogue listing all available Mystique Books,
send your name and address to:

MYSTIQUE BOOKS,
M.P.O. Box 707, Niagara Falls, N.Y. 14302
In Canada: 649 Ontario St., Stratford, Ontario N5A 6W2

Return to Foxdale

by LEO DARTEY

MYSTIQUE BOOKS

TORONTO • LONDON • NEW YORK
HAMBURG • AMSTERDAM

RETURN TO FOXDALE/first published February 1980

Copyright © 1980 by Worldwide Library
Copyright © MCMLXIV by Librairie Jules Tallandier, as
LA COLLINE AUX GENETS
Philippine copyright 1980. Australian copyright 1980.

ISBN 0-373-50066-1

PRINTED IN U.S.A.

Chapter 1

Caroline Mesner got off the subway at Hampstead, and by the time she reached the street, there was a jaunty bounce in her step. She was confident that she'd done well on her art exams and for the thousandth time in her twenty-two years she wondered if having artistic talent of any sort was hereditary. As far as she knew, no one on either side of her family had any talent for drawing or painting. Her father had been an engineer before he returned to Spain and contented himself with tending the garden in their villa near Barcelona. And her mother was *the* Vera Solane.

For more than twenty years, Vera Solane had been the world's leading operatic contralto, the darling of the world's capitals. *It's funny*, Caroline thought as she climbed up the hill past the small shops to the High Street. *Everyone in the world seems to know my mother better than I do.* But Caroline was accustomed to her unusual situation and had long since dispensed with trying to ferret out profound psychological explanations. For the past ten years she had lived with the Clarke family in a charming suburb of London, and she'd managed to put the pain of being an unwanted child behind her. Those tearful memories were more like remembered nightmares to her now: the details were still clear in her memory, but they could no longer hurt her.

Caroline had only been twelve when her beloved father had died, and almost immediately her mother had packed her off to live with the Clarkes in London. There had been no time in Vera Solane's life for a gawky twelve-year-old child, and Caroline hadn't seen her since.

She was more than grateful to the Clarkes. They were the only family she'd known over the past decade, and they'd been very good to her. Mr. Clarke had died before Caroline had gone to live with them, but Mrs. Clarke and her three children had accepted her as one of the family almost at once.

Walking past the park with its shimmering pond, Caroline paused for a moment to watch the children crouched by the water sailing their boats in the warm May sun. How simple their world seemed, and Caroline wondered if they knew how lucky they were to be growing up in a normal home with both parents. Caroline had vowed years before that when she was married and had children of her own, she would never turn them over to a governess or send them off to boarding school. She knew from her own experience that it was just too difficult for a child to comprehend being sent away. Too often it was interpreted as personal rejection.

But now, as she inhaled the fresh air of Hampstead

Heath and watched the crocuses, tulips and daffodils turning their blossoms toward the early afternoon sun, Caroline didn't want to think about such things. She was young, doing well in her studies, and in another year she would graduate from commercial art school and go into the world of business. Occasionally it occurred to her she might like to return to the United States, where she had been born, to launch her career. But she could hardly remember the country of her birth, and her failure to formally declare American citizenship before she was twenty-one, as she might have done, would make immigration difficult.

Her mother had been a first-generation American, born of Italian immigrant parents. At that time her name was Maria Costanza. Caroline had heard the story many times, yet never ceased to marvel at her mother's unswerving determination to become a world-famous opera singer. Apparently, back then it was unthinkable that a hopeful singer would retain her own name, and her mother had chosen the stage name, Vera Solane, because it sounded more impressive than her own.

The young Vera had denied herself any resemblance to a normal childhood. Instead, she practiced constantly and managed to win scholarships for voice lessons at the very best schools and with private tutors. Her whole world had been her voice and its perfection. The woman didn't even breathe like other people: every intake of air was carefully controlled to strengthen her diaphragm and improve her projection.

As Caroline turned the corner and strolled toward the Clarke home which stood among the well-tended row houses, she had to admit that she didn't possess her mother's dedication. She was far more like her easygoing English father who preferred puttering in his Spanish garden or reading Caroline stories rather than devoting himself to a career in engineering. "It's rather a lonely occupation," he'd once told her. "What you design and build will be used by people for generations to come, yet no one remembers your name or who built the damned thing. No, my pet, give me my flowers and my precious moments with you. That's all I really want."

"But what about mama?" she remembered asking, surprised at his choice.

Her father had smiled, then patted her soft brown hair. "Your mother is unique. I love her deeply, but she must be left free. Like a beautiful bird, she can't sing if she's kept in captivity."

Caroline had only been about nine or ten at the time, but his words had made her terribly sad. It was as if, at that moment, she finally understood that her mother was not like other people. She was more like a fairy princess who had to live by special rules or she would perish. It seemed so terrible to Caroline then—as if her mother was a veritable prisoner of the very freedom she required.

Caroline pushed her memories aside as she walked toward the house.

"Hello, Caroline," Mrs. Clarke called, waving from her kneeling position in the flower garden. "How were the exams?"

"Not at all bad," she answered, then laughed. "That, or I'm a fool and missed every one of the questions!"

"That's not likely, my love! You've a good head on your shoulders, and you've worked very hard. I'm sure you've done just splendidly." She turned her lightly lined face toward Caroline with mock admonishment. From her expression it was clear that she didn't like to be teased about anything so important. Then she smiled. "The tea's steeping and should be ready in a minute or two. John's upstairs. Give him a shout—he's promised to join us."

"Super." Caroline smiled. John, the eldest, had always been her favorite. Beneath the austere young physician's manner he was a gruff, but affectionate big brother to her. "What about Lucy and Anne?"

Mrs. Clarke sighed, waving her trowel. "Off to the movies again, I'm afraid. I swear I don't know whatever will become of those girls! Every penny they earn goes for afternoon movies, fan magazines and records of those awful rock singers.... I wouldn't doubt they'll be deaf before they're twenty! Wasteful, that's what it is," Mrs. Clarke muttered, returning her attention momentarily to a bit of crabgrass that she'd failed to weed out. "Oh, Caroline dear, I almost forgot...."

Caroline paused, one hand on the doorknob.

"You've a letter. It's on the sideboard."

"I do? But who on earth would write to me?"

Mrs. Clarke's round blue eyes squinted up at her. "I can't be sure, mind you, but I think it might be from your mother."

"But that's impossible," Caroline said, an uncertain tone in her voice. "Mother never writes to me. You know that."

"Yes, yes, I know," Jean Clarke said. "But still, there you are. It's from Spain. Who else do you know in Spain?"

Caroline tried to smile. "I'll soon find out," she said as she went into the cool, carpeted hallway.

The letter was on the sideboard as Jean Clarke had said it would be. The envelope was postmarked Bada-lona, a small town near the villa Caroline knew so well. Yet Caroline still couldn't believe her own eyes. In the ten years she'd been living with the Clarkes she hadn't received a single letter from her mother—only the ritual telegram at Christmas and a box of chocolates for her birthday. But who else would write her from Spain?

Spain. The mere word was enough to stir troubled emotions within her...mixed with some of her most cherished memories. Near a small Mediterranean town not far from Barcelona, her father had purchased an an-cient country estate called Valle de Zorro, or Foxdale in translation, awaiting her mother's return from trium-phant engagements and the few days she could spend with them, relaxing in preparation for the next whirl-wind tour.

Caroline had loved the estate. After being dragged from city to city and left with governesses for the first six years of her life, she was delighted when her father had made the decision to establish a permanent home for the family.

The following six years of her life had been spent with her father in the beautiful villa, surrounded by its wonderful gardens and expansive lawn overlooking the sea. She'd soon learned to speak Spanish almost as well as the natives, and had spent her days happily at the local school or, whenever possible, swimming in a secluded bay near the villa.

Caroline returned her thoughts to the present. Somewhat nervously, she picked up the pale green envelope and stared at her name scribbled on it. The stationery was faintly scented, but it had been too long since Caroline had seen her mother's handwriting for her to identify it. She opened the envelope and took out the matching paper, immediately glancing at the signature on the second page. It was her mother's.

Footsteps on the stairs behind her caused Caroline to look up and turn around. "Hi, Johnnie," she said nervously.

He paused at the bottom step, a slight frown on his face. His gray eyes scrutinized her beneath dark eyebrows. "It *is* from your mother, then?"

"Apparently, though I can't imagine why she's writing."

"I didn't mean to intrude, Caroline. I'll be outside with mother."

"No, no! Please, John, you're not intruding at all. In fact, I . . . well, I'm a bit scared to read what she has to say."

"And with good reason," he replied seriously. "The woman hasn't bothered to communicate with you for ten years, so I guess she must have something quite important to say."

Caroline extended the two pages of the letter to him. "Would you mind reading it to me, Johnnie? It's cowardly, I know, but . . . ."

He took the letter with a nod of agreement, then indicated that she should join him in the sitting room. He crossed over to the window for better light and began to read slowly, his voice somewhat tight.

"My dear child,

I don't even dare to think what your reaction might be at finally receiving a letter from your mother after such an unforgivably long silence. But please don't be too hasty in your judgment—let me try to explain. No doubt you think of me as a vain, selfish person, and I have little to say in my defense. Perhaps I am. All I can say is that I have spent my entire life singing; it has been as important to me as food and sleep are for others. Singing has always been the sum total of my existence—something your father always understood, and forgave. I hope, now that you are older, that I can make up to you all the years you've had to live without a mother—if you'll permit me.

You see, I am no longer singing. I, who was once known as "the voice of haunting velvet," have been forced to retire!"

John's eyebrows arched and he glanced over at Caroline suspiciously. "Had you heard anything about this before?"

"No," she answered simply. She was tempted to mention that she'd have no way of knowing. But she was aware of John's antagonism and decided to say nothing.

He nodded to himself and resumed reading.

"I won't bore you with the details now, dear Caroline, but the doctors say I will never sing again. I could have suffered an amputation of both legs with greater ease than this terrible blow. But I must face the truth and live with it as best I can.

I've been through some desperate moments and even considered taking my own life. However, about a month ago a friend suggested something that may be my salvation. I've come back to Foxdale and am in the process of restoring it to its former charm. Perhaps it's a foolish hope, but after all these years of living exclusively for my art, I now want to live a normal, quiet life. Foxdale was your father's haven from the world, and I remember well how very much you loved the old estate.

Which brings me to the reason for this letter. I want you to come home, Caroline. It's almost time for your summer holidays. Do you suppose we could spend them together, get to know each other all over again? There are so very many things I want to tell you, and perhaps more importantly, I want to see what kind of young lady you've become. I don't doubt for a moment that you must resent the way I packed you off after your father's death. I can't even beg you to think of me as your mother, in the traditional sense. But we could become friends, Caroline, and perhaps in time you might come to forgive me and love me...as I have always loved you, though I may have failed to show it.

Please write to me right away to let me know your decision. The thought of the two of us restoring Foxdale together is my only reason for living. You and this estate are all I really have to show for a life of denial. If you refuse to come, I don't know what I'll do."

John folded the letter neatly, shaking his head with a strangely hostile expression on his lean handsome face. "Of all the gall," he muttered. "She's still not putting you first—you're second to the damned house!"

"She must be terribly lonely," Caroline said, trying to keep the tears in her eyes from brimming over.

"A life of denial," John mimicked. "What has she lacked? The toast of Europe, the darling of the Americas! For her art, indeed! For her insatiable ego, that's what!"

"Oh Johnnie, please. You can't expect her to change overnight. Her only real mistake was in giving birth to me. Artists like mother should never have any children, but she did the best she knew how...and I had my father."

John ran his fingers through his brown curly hair. "You'll never stop defending her, will you, Caroline? I appreciate loyalty as much as anyone else, but your mother doesn't deserve it! Not now, not ever!"

"She's my mother—the only one I'll ever have."

He turned as his mother entered the room, a wary expression on her face. "I suppose," he began, watching his mother take the cozy off the teapot, "that means you'll be going."

Caroline had to smile at Mrs. Clarke's discretion as the woman silently poured the tea. She tactfully waited for Caroline's initiative in discussing the letter.

Briefly, Caroline told Mrs. Clarke what the letter had contained. As she spoke about her opportunity to go back to Spain, she felt a strange elation.

Nodding as she handed Caroline her tea, Mrs. Clarke said, "And of course you're accepting her invitation."

"Mother!"

"Well, why shouldn't she?" Mrs. Clarke asked logically. "I certainly hope, young man, that you'd want to see me, even if we'd been separated for ten years."

"Not if you'd abandoned me," he replied hotly.

"Oh, nonsense! We all do things at one time or another that we regret later. Stop being such a pompous young doctor and try to think with your heart for a change."

"That's just what I'm doing," he said a little more calmly. "I don't want to see Caroline hurt any more than she already has been."

"It's really quite simple," Mrs. Clarke said, taking a sandwich from the tray. "Either Caroline denies the existence of her mother, and passes up the chance to get to know the woman, or she takes her chances. As I've said before, there are only two ways it can possibly turn out: it'll either be all right, or it won't."

John smiled at the oft-repeated phrase then resumed his serious expression. "Yes, but what if it isn't all right this time?"

His mother cocked her head to one side, looking directly at Caroline. "Then Caroline will have a clear conscience. She will have given her mother the opportunity to make amends. What to do about it, if anything, will be Caroline's decision—not yours, not mine."

John crossed the room and picked up his teacup, a scowl still on his face. His mother turned to Caroline and asked, "Did she explain the nature of her illness?"

"No, I'm afraid not," Caroline replied.

"Well, I'll send you off with some of my special herb tea—that'll get her right as rain in no time."

Impulsively, Caroline put down her cup and leaned

toward Mrs. Clarke, hugging her affectionately. "You're terrific," she said gratefully.

Embarrassed, Mrs. Clarke concentrated on pouring herself another cup of tea.

Caroline glanced over at John, and for a moment saw an expression on his face she'd never seen before. He seemed worried, but perhaps even more peculiarly, he looked hurt—as if she were about to abandon him. But the moment he realized she was looking at him, he swiftly composed himself and began discussing how they would arrange for her trip to Badalona.

Chapter 2

Two weeks later Caroline disembarked from the Iberian Airlines jumbo jet and breathed the air of Barcelona. She followed the other passengers to the terminal, went through customs and presented her British passport to the very formal official. When she had last been in Spain, it had been controlled by *Generalísimo* Franco—savior to some, tyrant to others.

"Welcome to Spain, Miss Mesner," the official said, stamping her new blank passport with an elaborate rubber stamp.

"*Gracias*," she responded, smiling broadly at his expression of pleasant surprise. Though she'd made a point of studying Spanish in school so she wouldn't lose what she'd learned as a young girl, Caroline wasn't all that certain that her accent hadn't suffered from her British education. She was, she knew, a born mimic and unconsciously absorbed the inflections and usages of anyone around her.

Once beyond the gate, Caroline paused to reread the last letter from her mother saying that she'd be met by someone named Alejandro Martin, who was a deaf-mute and a trusted servant of many years.

As she scanned the crowds of travelers she was startled by a tap on her shoulder. Turning, she saw a wiry dark man in a chauffeur's uniform. He had a nasty scar that ran the length of his right cheek and, unsmiling, he presented a small pale green envelope to her. Caroline took it and removed the notepaper. The message was short, only confirming that the bearer was Alejandro and instructing her to go with him.

Smiling in what she hoped was a pleasant manner, she let the man take her two bulging suitcases, then followed him as he brusquely led the way through the terminal to the sedan waiting outside. It was a fairly new Peugeot, but had obviously traveled over some very dusty roads to reach the airport. Caroline wondered if, even after all these years, the streets of Badalona were still as bad as ever. Though only about a half-hour's drive up the coast from Barcelona, the small town stubbornly resisted progress.

Seated comfortably in the back seat, Caroline was glad that Alejandro drove a little more sedately than the average Spaniard. She leaned back and allowed her mind to wander back to the things she remembered about Badalona. She thought of the *plaza*, with its open-air market and boisterous crowds of vendors and fussy shoppers. And she recalled the wonderful fresh fish that were brought to the *plaza* daily and arranged in gaudy displays. How often she and her father had risen at dawn to walk down to the shore and watch the fishermen hauling in the catch of the day, the crisp, salty smell of seaweed blending with the breezes from the Mediterranean.

And the olives! There were no other olives like them in the entire world! Unfortunately, when they were exported, their aromatic oils had to be pasteurized, and the olives lost much of the flavor that made them so special. As a child she had bought them in small paper bags that always leaked and had eaten them like peanuts. And she and her father would often stop at one of the roadside carts selling *bacalao* cakes with a batter more delicate than any she'd ever tasted in London.

How happy she'd been then! Yes, she knew she had been different from other children—not only in nationality, but also because her mother had been so rarely at home. But her life had been filled with simple pleasures. . . .

Soon the sedan was skirting central Barcelona, and Caroline was surprised to see a new highway, as well as the hundreds of cars that traveled on it. The outskirts of the city and its industrial factories gradually gave way to small clusters of very poor houses as the road stretched parallel to the sea. Caroline vowed she'd take the train back to Barcelona once she settled in at Foxdale, just to see how much the city had changed and to revisit the wonderful museums. She never failed to be fascinated by the fact that Barcelona dated back to the second century, B.C. But excursions to Barcelona would have to wait until later; right now all she wanted to see was her beloved home.

The car began to climb the arid hills behind the town of Badelona, kicking dust and grit into the air as Alejan-

dro maneuvered it along the winding road. They
bumped and lurched past familiar landmarks and Caroline's excitement mounted with each passing one. She
remembered that tree and that monstrously huge boulder; and yes, over there to her left, the cluster of
cypresses just before the bend in the road that would
lead them directly to Foxdale. Even though she had been
nervous about seeing her mother again, wondering how
they'd get along, nothing could detract from her special
joy of coming home. It would seem strange to be there
without her father, but Caroline was sure she would feel
him nearby, pleased for her.

Then, as the road took a bend to the right, she could
see the estate. It was glistening white with fresh paint,
and its dark red-tile roof was overrun with brilliantly-
colored bougainvillea. She sighed with relief: the two-
story stucco house stood solidly on the promontory over
the sea just as she had remembered it.

She was tempted to say something to Alejandro, to
remark on how beautiful it still was, but then she
remembered he was deaf as well as mute. Moreover, his
stiff manner didn't encourage any familiarity. She would
just have to bear in mind that she was in Spain again,
where one did not fraternize with the employees.

As they pulled up to the front veranda, Caroline was
better able to see how the once carefully tended gardens
had become overrun and neglected. But this realization
was swiftly pushed aside as she saw her mother descending the front steps...majestically, regally, as if an
audience were awaiting her.

"My very dear child," Vera Solane said almost
theatrically, the flowing chiffon sleeves of her brightly

colored dress beckoning as she opened her arms to receive her daughter.

"You haven't changed a bit, mother," Caroline said, at once delighted and a little uncomfortable as her mother embraced her.

"Of course I have, Caroline, but that's sweet of you to say. I was a mere forty when you last saw me." With a rippling laugh, she put her arm around Caroline's shoulders. "Don't bother with your things, dear. Alejandro will bring them in."

When they reached the front door, Vera paused and turned toward Caroline. "Now, let's have a look at you.... Hmm, your father all over again," she said affectionately.

"His straight nose and eyebrows, but I have your eyes and mouth. At least, that's what father used to say."

Vera pursed her lips and scrutinized her daughter. "Yes, I suppose so. I've had three facelifts, my dear, and I may well have forgotten what I looked like at your age."

Caroline was taken aback. "Three? In only ten years?"

Her mother smiled a little self-consciously. "Well, not precisely, I suppose. I had my eyes done when I was in my late thirties, shortly before your father's death. Then, a whole facelift when I was forty-four, and another just this year to help me get a fresh outlook on life. When you're in the theater, Caroline, the makeup destroys your complexion and the hot lights bake your skin mercilessly. Then, as well we all know, one's fans— and the impressarios—want you to remain forever young. You can't have a fifty-year-old singing the part of Carmen!"

"But you don't look a day over thirty-five," Caroline protested sincerely. "Besides, I always thought that part was sung by a mezzo-soprano."

"First, my plastic surgeon thanks you, and second, Carmen usually is sung by a mezzo. But what has that got to do with what Vera Solane can do?"

Caroline merely shook her head, enchanted as ever by her mother's wonderfully lyrical speaking voice, her deep throaty laugh and the utter femininity of her every practiced gesture. Perhaps Vera Solane was no longer singing in theaters, but she was still obviously very much on stage.

"Now," her mother said as they entered the cool, tile-floored foyer, "you must bear with me, Caroline. Getting this old place back to its former magnificence is a much bigger job than I'd anticipated, and most of the house is still in a shambles. However, the most-used rooms have been restored, and particularly—"

"My bedroom?" Caroline interrupted eagerly.

Vera's perfectly molded red lips broke into a smile revealing incredibly white teeth. "Especially your room," she said. "The moment you wrote to say you were coming, I had the workers start on it at once. I thought you'd prefer to stay there rather than upstairs. Besides, it's cooler than downstairs. I daresay all your years in England have thinned your blood, and you'll feel our heat more than you used to."

For a split second Caroline resented her mother's reference to "our heat." She had rarely stayed at the villa for more than a few days, while Caroline had been brought up there, growing like a weed in the warm climate. But the resentment passed almost as quickly as it had come.

If it made her mother happy to think that everything about Foxdale was exclusively hers, what harm could come of it?

They entered the living room and Caroline stopped in her tracks. "It's different," she murmured quietly.

"Oh, yes, of course it is! I've had it enlarged—it was always much too small for a decent party."

"But even the furniture...."

"Darling, you wouldn't want me to invite nobility and the greatest names in music and the arts to a provincial country hovel, would you?" Vera patted her daughter's shoulder and moved to the magnificent floor-to-ceiling window that overlooked the Mediterranean. "Come, the vista hasn't changed," Vera said soothingly, extending her hand.

Slowly, almost cautiously, Caroline walked toward the window. As always, the view made her catch her breath. Down below, were the rooftops of Badalona; out beyond, the glittering, gentle sea mirrored the burnt-orange globe of the late-afternoon sun. At this time of year the sun wouldn't set fully much before nine o'clock, but the late-day breezes were already playing with the trees. Low, cottony-white clouds hovered to the west almost like a pillow to cushion the sun's descent.

"I've thought of this view so many times," Caroline whispered. "At first, when I went to live with the Clarkes, the memory of this scene was the only thing that kept me going."

As if from a great distance, Vera said, "Were you really that miserable?"

Tears stung at Caroline's eyes. "Yes, desperately. I'd never known you, but I'd lost my father and this home, and was sent off to strangers in damp, overcast London. It hurt a great deal."

"But you were just a child, Caroline! Children adapt very quickly to new surroundings."

Caroline tried to smile when she turned to look at her beautiful mother. "I can't speak for other children, but perhaps that's true when they feel secure—when they're with their parents and believe everything will be all right."

"Poor darling," Vera said sympathetically. "I only hope to be able to make it up to you . . . somehow."

A light rapping at the archway to the foyer interrupted them. "Excuse me, Vera, but I need your signature for the workmen's paychecks."

"Oh, Patrick, I'm glad you're here," Vera said, her whole mood changing to that of the gracious hostess. "I want you to meet my daughter, Caroline Mesner."

The young man who came forward was about six feet tall, with very broad muscular shoulders that tapered into a firm waist. His hair was thick and black and sharply defined by a pronounced widow's peak .His eyebrows arched above clear hazel eyes. "How do you do," he said from the archway.

"Caroline, this is Pat O'Flaherty. He's consented to oversee the renovations and additions ."

"How do you do," she repeated, feeling somewhat uncomfortable under his piercing gaze.

Pat handed Vera the large ledger containing the payroll checks and watched her idly as she crossed to the large Louis XVI desk at the other end of the room. "Will you be visiting long, Miss Mesner?" he asked after a moment.

"For the summer holidays," she answered, wondering why this young man had such an air of proprietary confidence about him. She wasn't at all keen about the way he addressed her mother by her first name.

"Good, then I guess we'll be seeing quite a bit of each other. I could even show you some of our local sights, if you wish."

"Here you are, Pat," Vera said, handing the ledger back to him as she rejoined them. "Are you off, then?"

"Yes," he replied, smiling easily. "I have to drive into Barcelona and see about getting some new plumbing fixtures. The ones you have now are antiquated."

"Off you go, then. We'll see you tomorrow, I suppose."

Though Caroline couldn't put her finger on it, there was definitely something more than just an employer-employee relationship between her mother and this young man.

"He's a nice young man, Caroline, and I'm sure you two will have a great deal to talk about once you get to know each other. But for tonight, it's just the two of us."

"I beg your pardon?" Caroline's mind was still on the man who'd just left the living room.

Vera smiled. "I gave all of the servants the night off so we could be alone and catch up with one another. Of course, not being a cook, I did prevail on Señora Mendez to prepare something special for your first night at home."

"*Paella* by any chance? It was always my favorite dish!"

"Naturally. I'm your mother, after all. Besides, all I

have to do is heat it up," she added conspiratorially. "Would you like a cocktail first?"

"Not for me, thanks. Maybe a glass of wine. But you go ahead," Caroline said, dimly aware of the sound of a car's engine starting up in the distance. "This Pat O'Flaherty," she said hesitantly as she watched her mother taking ice cubes from a crystal bucket.

"Yes? What about Pat?"

"Is . . . is he a salaried contractor here?"

Vera turned around, wreathed in smiles. "Find him attractive already? Well, actually, Pat's a bit more than just the hired help at Foxdale," she continued hesitantly, then paused. "But let's not talk about him now when we have so much catching up to do."

Caroline sensed that her mother didn't want to discuss the subject of Patrick O'Flaherty. Although she would have liked to have discovered more about him and his relationship with her mother, she let the matter drop. "When did you start drinking?" she asked, suddenly remembering that her mother had always abstained from alcohol.

Vera shrugged. "When the doctors said my career was over, finished, a dead issue. I've even been learning to smoke," she added, a mildly amused look in her dark eyes. "If I can't have my greatest joy, I may as well have all the vices."

"But that's so unlike you, mother," Caroline said, surprised but not judgmental.

"How would you know, dear?"

Caroline smiled slowly. "You're right, I wouldn't." Then her attention was caught by a painting on the wall behind her mother. "Isn't that a Cézanne?" she asked, moving toward it to get a better look.

"A copy of one, yes. Are you interested in art, Caroline?"

Caroline looked at her mother in disbelief until it dawned on her that, of course, she would have no way of knowing that Caroline had been at art school for the last two years. Not allowing herself to be hurt by her mother's ignorance and keeping her tone conversational, Caroline told Vera Solane about her studies and what she hoped to achieve once she graduated.

"I'm doing rather well, actually," she said shyly, but with a note of pride in her voice. As she spoke she glanced at the other copies in the room, all of them of masters she recognized immediately.

"Of course, the real test will be when I graduate and have to get a job," she went on. "The market for graduate commercial artists is pretty tight right now; there's a tremendous amount of competition."

"It'll be good for you," Vera said, handing Caroline a glass of white wine. "We all need challenges in order to do our best."

"Yes, but first you have to be given the chance to prove what you can do...and that's the problem nowadays."

"I'm not worried about you," Vera said, lifting her glass and indicating she was about to give a toast. "To us, Caroline. To mother and daughter, reunited at long last, and to the friendship I know we'll have."

"Nothing would please me more," Caroline answered warmly. She sipped from her glass and noticed again how remarkably well her mother had retained her youthful appearance, facelift or not. Had she wanted to, Vera Solane could have passed as Caroline's older sister, and no one would have been the wiser.

In an attempt to keep the conversation from flagging, Caroline changed the subject to the paintings in the room. "I didn't know you were such an art collector. When did you develop a taste for the Impressionists?"

Vera's expression clouded over for a second. "Actually, it's not my collection, as such. I asked Pat's uncle to help me decorate this room, and he got these copies for a song."

"Well, he certainly has excellent taste. Is Pat's uncle a friend of yours—is that what you meant about Pat being more than just a contractor?"

"More or less," she hedged. "But let's let all that wait till tomorrow, Caroline. Right now, I want to hear about everything you've been up to for the past ten years. What school was like, what you wore on your first date...things like that."

"Do you really expect me to remember?" Caroline asked, smiling.

"Of course! That's why you went to live with the Clarkes—so you could have the childhood I never had. Now I want to know all about it."

There was such an expression of anticipated pleasure on her mother's face that Caroline almost felt as if she were talking to a school friend. At first, she merely summarized the highlights of her life in England, such as they were. She told her mother about Lucy, Anne and John, and about how very good and kind Mrs. Clarke had been to her.

"John," her mother mused. "Yes, I remember now. He was the oldest boy, as I recall."

"The only son," Caroline amended. "And now he's a doctor. Quite a good one, or so he'd have you believe."

"Do I hear a hint of romance in your voice?"

"Oh, mother," Caroline said lightly, "you just can't help finding drama in everything, can you," she teased. "No, there's nothing between us besides friendship."

"Hmm, that's what I said before I agreed to marry your father," she said in an amused voice. "Well, life is a drama. The only difference is that we have little control over the plot in real life. Perhaps this young man means more to you than you think."

"I doubt it," Caroline replied, knowing she'd never considered John in any light other than as a big brother. Had he thought of her differently? She wondered. . . .

Chapter 3

By the time they'd finished supper and had stacked the dishes neatly in the kitchen for the maid to wash in the morning, Caroline felt relaxed and at ease. While she couldn't say that she was totally won over by her mother's warm charm, Caroline knew that any reservations she had were mostly due to the unspoken resentments left over from her childhood. In time, perhaps, she would be able to relate to Vera Solane as a friend and maybe even as a mother. As it was, right now she was finding it difficult to get past the image of the famous opera star playing the part of doting mother, twenty-two years after the fact.

"You know, mother, I'm really quite impressed with how you've adapted to life on a Spanish estate. From your first letter, I expected to find you pining away on a chaise longe, playing your own recordings and dabbing at your eyes with a lace hanky."

Vera lifted her coffee cup and had a faraway expression in her eyes. "If you hadn't agreed to come, that might well have happened."

Caroline shook her head. "No, really. Look what you've managed to accomplish in only a month and a half! Granted, not all of the house has been restored, but much of it has. As for the grounds, they'll be beautiful again in no time. What about the vineyards? Were they also abandoned?" Caroline could have kicked herself the moment the last word was spoken, but it was too late and she only hoped her mother wouldn't notice.

"Oh, darling, everything here was a shambles when I came back. It looked like one huge inverted bird's nest. Brambles, weeds.... Ten years is a long time to leave a place untended," she continued.

"Then all the more reason to feel proud of yourself," Caroline said cheerfully. "Have you begun to cultivate the land...and what about old Señor Ortega? Have you hired him back to oversee the vineyards?"

Vera hesitated briefly. "Señor Ortega died a few years ago, Caroline. He was very old and had lived a good life." Vera extended her left hand and patted Caroline's consolingly. "But," she resumed, "we've decided to mechanize and modernize the entire operation. The lands will be cleared, and then we'll bring in modern presses and bottling equipment. In winemaking, as in any other business, efficiency is the key to profits!"

Caroline wasn't surprised to learn that the old overseer had died; even ten years ago he had hardly been able to get around. But something else was bothering her. "We? Who's we, mother?"

Vera frowned momentarily, then she looked down at

her cup. "I hadn't wanted to discuss this on your first evening back, but I suppose I really should."

Curious and somewhat apprehensive, Caroline watched her mother rise from the table and take the tray of liqueurs from the sideboard.

"You may as well know, I suppose," she began a little nervously. "You see, my dear, I'm broke."

"What?"

"No, listen to me, please. I've made an enormous amount of money over the years, it's true, but there's none left. People think an opera star appears on stage, sings her part and goes off to fancy cocktail parties with admiring fans. The truth of the matter is that it's a life of constant work. I've had to continue to study, as all singers do. Then there's the expense of paying a pianist to accompany me and the cost of gowns for concert tours. Whereas you can walk into any department store and buy any dress that suits you, I must have couturier clothes—it's expected of me. Entertaining is a very large part of this life, and that, too, is a frightening expense."

"And paying for my room and board at the Clarkes'," Caroline interjected, hardly able to believe that her mother could have spent all her earnings.

Vera waved aside the comment. "The point is, it has cost me almost as much as I've earned to sustain the life of a star. What little I had left when I was told I had to retire has been put into a modest trust fund."

"But," Caroline interrupted, "all this!" Her gesture included the extensive restoration and rebuilding that had been done to the estate. "Walls knocked out, rooms extended, additional wings added.... I don't mean to pry, mother, but the work that's been done here will cost a fortune! And you're not even through yet."

"I know, Caroline, I know," her mother said guardedly.

"Then, how . . . ?"

Her mother lifted a bottle of cognac, and when Caroline shook her head, poured some into a snifter for herself. "I don't expect you to fully understand, dear," Vera said hesitantly. "Sometimes we must do things in our lives that . . . well, we might not do if circumstances were different."

"Mother, please get to the point," she said as gently as her impatience allowed her.

The woman raised her shoulders philosophically. "A gentleman I met about two years ago . . . an ardent admirer of mine. . . ."

"Go on, mother."

Vera's eyebrows rose, and she seemed to be searching for words. "He had been proposing to me for more than a year. He's a good man, Caroline, but if you don't know him well, he can seem quite cold and indifferent. At your age, I don't expect you to accept the notion of a marriage of convenience. But at my age, and in my financial straits—with no hope of a career ahead of me—it was a sensible decision. Let us just say that he's cultured and enormously wealthy."

Caroline could only stare at her mother. It wasn't that she had never heard of a woman marrying for security; it was more that it seemed the last thing in the world her mother would ever have to do. Naturally, Caroline instantly thought of her father, wondering what he might think about this development. But Caroline realized that after ten years her mother was entitled to remarry—to find companionship, even love. "So it is this man's fortune that is restoring Foxdale."

"Yes. I could never have done it myself, and it was his suggestion, Caroline, that you come home, that we get to know each other all over again and that the two of us rebuild the villa."

"I see. And when did the marriage take place?"

"About five months ago, when the doctors started to warn me that I might never sing again. Victor pleaded with me to marry him. He adores me, Caroline, and that counts for a great deal at my age," she said with a plea in her voice.

"Please stop talking about your age, mother. You don't look it, and you're obviously not exactly bedridden with illness." Caroline was unable to keep a slight reproof out of her voice, and she was surprised to see that her mother seemed hurt.

"You hate me for betraying your father's memory, don't you?" Vera asked simply, tears welling in her eyes.

Caroline fought in vain to keep her anger in check. "No, mother, I don't hate you. I don't think I ever could. If I haven't hated you for dumping me with strangers, then it's not likely to happen now," she said letting out years of pent-up bitterness. "But you're so childlike," Caroline continued unable to control her frustration. "I don't understand why you just didn't tell me that you'd remarried. For that matter, why didn't you invite me to the wedding? I just don't understand you, I guess."

Vera's large dark-brown eyes were overflowing with tears and her chin began to quiver. "I never meant to hurt you, Caroline. I thought it would be easier for you if you lived in a normal atmosphere, around ordinary people. I'd have written. . . . I meant to, many times, but somehow the time always got away from me. Rehearsals, performances, dance lessons to stay limber and in shape. There was always something to interfere!"

"What about the hours on airplanes, on trains or even in hotel rooms? Couldn't you have written then? Didn't you ever wonder how I was? Couldn't you have phoned?"

"Caroline, you just don't understand! I never had the time!"

"Time? You know, mother, I once had an algebra teacher who taught me a valuable lesson. Whenever someone in the class would use lack of time for an excuse not to have done homework, he'd bellow: 'Time? You've lots of time. There are twenty-four hours in a day! You simply preferred to do something else, like eat or sleep or work out for the soccer team—but there was plenty of time!' Beneath your glamorous facade, you've never really grown up, mother."

Vera buried her face in her hands, taking deep breaths, then looked up at her daughter. "I don't know what to say," she whispered.

"I doubt that there's anything you can say," Caroline said quietly. It grieved her to see her mother so upset, but the words had poured out like water from a broken dam. She hadn't meant to bring up the way her mother had packed her off, but somehow the fact that her mother had once again shut Caroline out of her life by marrying without telling her own daughter had triggered a response in Caroline that she couldn't control.

"Oh Caroline, I am terribly sorry. You're right, of

course, there can be no excuse for the way I ignored you. Can you ever forgive me?"

Caroline rose and walked around the table to her mother's hunched form. Placing her arms around the woman, Caroline spoke soothingly, trying to stem the tears. "Why don't we start all over again? From here on in, no games, no surprises, not even a hint of keeping things from each other. That will be a big step in the right direction."

"Yes. I know that would be best," Vera agreed, her voice trembling. She dabbed at her eyes with the edge of her napkin and straightened her shoulders. "You're really very mature for someone your age," she said with a feeble smile.

Caroline smiled back at her. "Just remember, mother, that life isn't the theater.... You don't have to hold things back for the most dramatic moment. All right?"

"You make me feel as if you're the mother and I'm the child," Vera said, slowly regaining her composure. Then she paused before adding, "If we're to be completely truthful, I should say one more thing. I think you should know that Victor wanted you to be present for our wedding. I believed it would upset you terribly, and I insisted that I tell you later on, when we'd had a chance to get to know each other again."

"That was considerate of Victor," Caroline said. "I only wish you'd listened to him."

"Well, later, when we began to restore the estate, it was again Victor who suggested you come here to be a part of it. I thought it would be better to wait until it was all done, so you wouldn't be shocked at how run-down it was. But Victor won out, as you can tell."

Caroline's voice was light and jocular as she asked, "And does Victor have a last name? Where is he, by the way?"

Her mother smiled radiantly, all traces of her former upset gone. "He's in Paris on business, but he'll be home Sunday afternoon. His name is Victor O'Flaherty, and he's an art dealer."

"O'Flaherty," Caroline repeated. "Then, he's. . . ."

"Pat's uncle. Yes, darling. Pat lives here with us."

"Does he plan to stay, even after the estate has been restored?" Caroline couldn't quite adjust to this new information. Although Badalona was only an hour's drive from Barcelona, she wondered why a young man would want to spend his time in such a provincial town.

Vera poured another brandy for herself and blinked several times as if to try to understand the question. "I don't know, dear. It's never come up. Pat does seem very fond of Foxdale and of course he reveres his uncle. Victor has treated him like a son all his life, giving him the best of everything."

The irony of the situation wasn't lost on Caroline. This young man owed everything to his uncle, while she had a mother she didn't even know.

CAROLINE SLEPT FITFULLY that night, rousing from time to time to remember bits and pieces of her conversation with her mother and weaving the Clarkes and Patrick O'Flaherty into her dreams. Somehow, even her childhood seemed a part of the unconscious mosaic.

But in the morning, as the early rays of the sun crept through her windows, she awakened feeling better, as if the last hour or two of sleep had been enough rest. She lay in bed, reliving her life in that room in the quiet moments before rising. She remembered her father selecting the wallpaper, an Australian print, with stags leaping over fallen trees, chalets in snow and drawings of forests with the sun tipping the treetops. She later decided he had chosen it to remind her that there was another world beyond Badalona, and remembered she had spent many a morning imagining herself frolicking among those images.

The window in her room looked out onto a small, almost private, courtyard. Richly colored vines covered the whitewashed walls, and flowers and ferns were planted strategically to delight the eye. Surrounded by three walls, the flowers gave off a heady scent each morning, which was mixed with the tangy salt air from the Mediterranean. It was enough to give anyone a very hearty morning appetite, and today was no different.

Hoping that the cook, Señora Mendez, had arrived, Caroline threw off the light coverlet on her bed and padded to the adjoining bathroom. She caught a glimpse of herself in the mirror and stopped to examine herself. In some ways she did look like her mother; in others, there was little or no resemblance. Her dark straight eyebrows had none of the dramatic effect of her mother's arched brows. Her nose, just a little too short for Caroline's taste, was definitely her father's. But the large, velvety brown eyes...yes, those were the same eyes as Vera Solane's. So was the mouth, a little wider than fashion preferred, but full and ready to smile.

The primary difference, Caroline thought, was that she still had the fullness of youth, whereas her mother's face had thinned down, revealing interesting cheekbones and planes.

Caroline smiled at her reflection. "When you're through gawking, Miss Mesner, perhaps you'd be good enough to dress and go downstairs," she addressed her reflection.

Half an hour later, she pushed open the swinging door to the huge country kitchen. She had marveled the night before at its modernization and was struck again by the efficiency of the refrigerator and electric stove. Gas was not commonly used outside the larger cities, and before the kitchen had been remodeled, the kitchen had contained a butane tank to supply the necessary fuel. How long ago that all seemed . . . another lifetime.

"Good morning," she said cheerily to the woman standing at the sink cracking ranch-fresh eggs.

"*Ay, señorita*, welcome," the woman said, bowing her head and smiling. "I am Señora Mendez and this is Consuelo," she continued, pointing to her helper.

Caroline nodded, then smiled at the teenage girl peeling onions at the square kitchen table.

"You are hungry?" Señora Mendez asked.

"Yes, famished," Caroline answered. "But I can wait for my mother to come downstairs."

The woman looked heavenward good-naturedly. "Then you are waiting for a long time, *señorita*. Your *mamacita* does not sing with the birds in the morning! Come, I will fix you something now."

"Thank you," Caroline said, smiling. She helped herself to the round loaf of oven-baked bread on the counter and cut off a thin slice. Then she lifted the lid off the skillet where the spicy sausages were frying. "The sausages smell divine," she said. "I haven't had *chorizo* in ten years!"

Señora Mendez shrugged. "I am still not used to electricity, that creation of the devil! Woodstoves, yes; gas, yes. But I do not understand this electricity that makes heat without a fire. How is one to know how hot it is?"

Caroline laughed easily. "By what it says on the dial," she explained.

"Ah, but how does a dial know? Eh? It is not right that a machine know more than what I can see for myself. Bah!"

Caroline didn't bother to try to explain the principles of electricity. Instead, she sat down opposite Consuelo as the cook poured half a cup of pan-brewed coffee into a large deep bowl and filled the rest with the simmering milk from the stove. Caroline sighed, savoring the moment when she could sip the hot liquid with the cream thickened into a thin film over it. She remembered that her father had always hated the film, or *nata*. He would have the cook skim it off the top of the heated milk and give it to Caroline, who loved it.

Suddenly the back door opened, and Pat O'Flaherty was standing there, wiping his boots off on the doormat. "Well, good morning," he said with just a hint of an Irish lilt in his voice. "Are you always an early riser, or just today?"

"Usually I am," she answered, a little amused to see Consuelo blush at his appearance, then rush to get him a cup of coffee. "Are you just getting back from Barcelona?"

"Me? No, I've been back almost two hours. There's a lot of work to be done around here, and if I don't see to it, it may not get done."

The cook brought them each a plate of sausages and eggs, and Consuelo placed a platter of bread between them.

"I see that Mrs. Mendez has already informed you that Vera doesn't get up until much later," he said as he bit into a sausage. Then he turned toward the cook. "These are delicious, Señora Mendez. I'd starve to death if it weren't for you."

The woman smiled. "You enjoy my simple food because you are working so hard, Señor Oflati."

Pat grinned and corrected her. "O'Flaherty. Come on, you can say it. Try."

She frowned at him, then shook her head. "It's an impossible name, *señor*," she said, dismissing him with a smile.

He looked affectionately at her from beneath his eyebrows as he tasted his eggs. "You'll come to appreciate the cook, too, Miss Mesner. She'll win you over with just a few meals."

"She already has," Caroline replied, liking him better after observing his fondness for the cook. "And please," she added, "call me Caroline."

His smile was impish. "I certainly will, provided you let me show you around after breakfast."

"That's a deal, Pat," she said, noticing for the first time his broad tanned hands—hands that worked for a living.

Chapter 4

The sun was beginning to warm the morning air as Caroline and Pat left the kitchen for their tour of the grounds. Fortunately, Caroline had put on a pair of low-heeled shoes, having planned to take a walk during the morning anyhow. They made her conscious of the fact that, at five-foot-four, she only came to Pat's shoulder and had to look up whenever he spoke to her.

"You're a good sport, Caroline, and I know Mrs. Mendez was pleased."

"About what?" she asked, pushing aside a tangle of dead vines so they wouldn't tear her linen slacks.

"Eating in the kitchen instead of insisting on being served in the dining room. She would've done it, of course, but you made her life easier, and I know she appreciates small things like that."

She gazed up at him, surprised. "You must be joking," she said, puzzled. "Why on earth would I insist on being served formally?"

His grin was immediate. "I see you weren't raised to be a spoiled brat," he said.

Caroline had to laugh. "Apparently mother hasn't told you that I was shipped off to a very proper middle-class English home where no one received any special privileges."

"Not even the daughter of Vera Solane?"

"Certainly not," she replied, trying to imagine Mrs. Clarke being deferential toward her. It was impossible to imagine such an attitude from the woman, and even more ridiculous to contemplate Lucy, Anne or John giving her special treatment.

They walked in silence for a way, and Caroline mentally tried to reconstruct what the gardens had looked like when she had been a little girl. About a hundred yards away, she was pleased to note the familiar grove of cork oaks shading the wooden structure that housed the wine presses. She knew that hundreds of woven baskets would be stacked nearly to the ceiling inside the building, and that all the ancient equipment would be stored there, in readiness to produce the better wines of the Rioja region. Rumor had it, Caroline remembered, that the present Foxdale estate had centuries before belonged to a Roman nobleman who had begun his own winery in the time of Caesar.

"You won't recognize this area in another couple of months," Pat said, following her gaze.

"Mother mentioned that you plan to modernize the equipment," she said, her eyes misting as she took in the rows and rows of gnarled vineyards, brown and dry from neglect.

"No more of those primitive implements stacked all

over the place. Instead of the old wooden wine press, we'll get a gleaming aluminum one that's fully mechanized and capable of pressing twenty times as many grapes."

"Will it affect the flavor of the wine?" she asked.

"Not so you'd notice. We plan to blend the wines."

"Blend them!" Caroline said, aghast.

"Why not? These Rioja wines aren't exactly in the same class as a Bordeaux. If one pressing is weak, we can blend it with a better one and sell both at a highly competitive price. Then," he said, gesturing broadly to the expanse on his left, "one day we'll put in our own automated bottling plant over there. Within five or six years, I want this place to be a totally vertical operation."

"Vertical meaning what?" She tried to sound politely interested, but was still shocked by Pat's plans to tamper with the wines. When her father was alive, he had kept the inferior wines for their own consumption and had sold the better ones to the local merchants. True, he'd never bothered to turn the winery into a money-making enterprise, but he'd always insisted that even a rough wine—as long as it was honest and pure— had more nobility than the blended ones. "If you take from the good to mix with the bad, you have mediocre wine," he had told her once.

But Caroline didn't know Pat O'Flaherty well enough to start repeating her father's theories, and she certainly didn't know enough about winemaking to back up arguments. Then Pat's reply to her earlier question brought her mind back to the present.

"It's the only smart way to go," he was saying. "By vertical, I mean that we'll own our own vineyards, ferment and store everything ourselves, then bottle and cork the wine right here. No middlemen, no reliance on outside suppliers or services. That way, we can keep the cost to a minimum and export at a profit."

Once again she found herself becoming annoyed at his proprietary attitude and wondered if he talked so confidently because it was his uncle's money that had made it all possible. But even if that was so, it wasn't Pat's money. Technically, he had no more right to the estate or its future than she did. Or was there more going on than her mother had revealed last night? Had she turned over the property to Victor O'Flaherty? Could she have done such a thing, knowing how very much Caroline loved the place?

"You seem very sure that this will be a financial bonanza," Caroline said, carefully seating herself on a rock beneath a tree.

Pat grinned and sat down next to her, plucking a blade of dry grass and putting it between his lips. "Why not? The cork oaks are already here, so we won't have to import cork from Portugal. And, other than bottles, about the only thing we'll have to buy is our labels. Victor and I have been talking about it, and we rather like the idea of calling our wines 'Rioja de Zorro.' What do you think?"

Caroline found her anger mounting, and even though she knew she had no right to interfere, she couldn't prevent herself from saying, "It seems to me that you and your uncle have pretty well decided what's going to happen around here. Why ask my opinion? I'm only a houseguest!" She got to her feet and had taken a step when Pat stood and forcibly turned her around.

"What's gotten into you?" he asked, half smiling.

"Nothing," she said tightly. Then she found herself blurting out her anger. "I come back to my childhood home and find that my mother has married someone I never heard of and have never met, and now you're telling me how this entire place is going to be revolutionized into a commerical operation within a few years. I suppose it's none of my business. After all Foxdale belongs to my mother, and she can do anything she wants with it. Or, at least, it used to belong to her," she concluded uncertainly.

Pat took the blade of grass from his lips and threw it to the ground, his hazel eyes expressing a combination of compassion and exasperation. "Look, I can understand that all this must have been quite a shock to you, but don't take it out on me. I wasn't the one who failed you."

"If you're referring to my mother, you're walking on thin ice," Caroline said, her dark brown eyes flashing up at him.

"Okay, forget the past. Let's talk about the present," he said, gripping her arm. "Your mother didn't have the money to rebuild this place, much less turn it into a viable business. Marrying my uncle gave her an opportunity she might otherwise never have had!"

Caroline's eyes narrowed and she could feel her temples beginning to throb. "Are you insinuating that she married Victor solely for his money?"

"You said it, I didn't," Pat replied, still holding onto her arm tightly.

"You're not only insolent," she murmured, almost unable to get the words out, "but you're despicable. How dare you!"

"Look, don't get all puffed up. I don't mean anything bad, Caroline. Victor adores Vera, and she needs him— what's wrong with that?"

A disdainful smile crossed her face. "Aren't you

changing your tune? Moments ago you were accusing my mother of failing me and of being little more than a money-grubbing female. Now you're turning things around and saying there's nothing wrong with it."

Pat's exasperation with her was obvious, but he was plainly trying to make amends. "It's only my damned Irish tongue," he said apologetically. "I didn't mean to make it sound that way. If you knew me better, you'd know that I was only being blunt, not malicious."

"Well, I *don't* know you better, Mr. O'Flaherty! And here I thought the Irish were noted for their winning ways and charm!" She started to pull away from his grasp, but winced when his grip tightened around her arm.

"The Irish are not all cut out of the same mold, Miss Mesner," he said softly, pulling her toward him. "But as long as you're going to be angry with me, I may as well give you a good reason!"

She felt herself being drawn to him, knowing what he was going to do and yet not quite able to believe it. When his face was a scant inch or two from hers, his breath warm against her eyes, she could feel the hard muscles of his chest through his thin cotton shirt. Seconds later, too shocked to protest and entirely at the mercy of his incredibly strong arms, Caroline felt Pat's lips touching hers.

His arms tightened around her, pulling her even more closely to him, as his lips melded against hers, pressing firmly as if to burn an imprint on her that would last forever.

Against her will, Caroline found herself responding to his kiss, to the raw strength and audacity of the man. Then, as his lips tried to part hers, she realized she was losing control. With a sudden push she managed to break away from him. Her breath was ragged as she stared at his amused face, and she felt humiliated for not having struggled against him sooner.

With his hands on his hips and an easy grin on his lips, he returned her stare. "Now that's Irish charm," he said slowly.

Caroline was entirely too angry to find any suitable retort. In an attempt to salvage what remained of her dignity, she turned abruptly and began to walk quickly back to the house.

His bold laughter broke the quiet like a clap of thunder in a summer storm.

SHE RACED UPSTAIRS as if pursued, only realizing when she reached the second floor, that she had no idea which room her mother would be in. It didn't seem likely that she would be in the same room that she had shared with her first husband, though Caroline suspected this would be because of Victor's insistence, rather than her mother's sensibilities.

"Mother?" she called tentatively, her fury now under control.

"In here, Caroline."

"In *where*, mother?" she asked, trying to pinpoint the direction of the woman's voice.

"Oh, yes, of course," Vera remarked, then laughed apologetically. "Where the guestroom used to be, darling."

Caroline turned to her right and headed down the wide hallway. As she did, she noticed how the passageway had been changed. Now there were windows and columns along the wall that faced the sea, giving the space the feeling of a loggia instead of a hall, while paintings and tapestries lined the other wall. Caroline briefly wondered why her mother had chosen the room farthest from the stairs. When she opened the door, it became obvious why Vera liked the room. It had been enlarged into a lovely private suite.

Vera sat at a round marble-topped table in an alcove that overlooked the Mediterranean. She was wearing a pale green peignoir, and her almost black hair was pulled back by a scarf with a subdued fernlike design. There were croissants and various marmalades before her on the table as well as a dull, pitted antique silver coffee carafe, accompanied by a Limoges china service. Vera Solane appeared to be the embodiment of the prima donna having her morning coffee in gracious surroundings, ready for the photographs from a leading magazine.

Had it been someone else, Caroline might have found it amusing, or even affected. But her mother needed these trappings, she now knew. Although it was highly unlikely that anyone would drop in, Vera had to live her role every minute of the day.

"Good morning, mother," she said, taking the chair opposite her. "Am I intruding upon you too early?"

"No, darling, of course not. I was just reading the reviews of the new staging of *Il Trovatore.* I used to adore playing Azucena—it was so wonderfully tragic!"

"Was it well received?" Caroline asked the question to show her interest, even though she found it difficult to feign enthusiasm for her mother's answer. All that opera meant to her was the vehicle that had robbed her of a mother.

"Oh, you know how these things are," Vera said almost

cheerfully. "People hate to break with tradition, and when they try a new staging of an old classic there's always a great deal of bickering from the critics. I remember when we did an entirely new production of *Macbeth* at the Met. Everything about it was planned except my performance. 'Brilliant,' they called it. 'Solane has exceeded even herself,' is what the *London Times* said. But then, you have to remember that the part of Lady Macbeth is generally given to a dramatic soprano. For a contralto to do it successfully...." Vera stopped short and smiled contritely. "I'm sorry, my dear. I do go on sometimes, and I forget that not everyone is interested."

"I'm sure you were fabulous, mother," Caroline said sincerely.

"Yes, well, all that's past now. However, you can appreciate how much training I've had over the years to handle the part. I doubt that there's another contralto alive today who could even carry it off, much less stun the critics."

Caroline was tempted to sympathize with her mother, but feared she would just set her off on another tangent about her precious, lost world. Instead, she patted her mother's hand and smiling, said, "You achieved what few others have, isn't that enough? Isn't it time to let someone else try to become as great as you?"

Vera's laugh was almost a titter. "Let them try! A superb contralto is a rarity. If one comes along each generation, the music world is grateful."

Caroline refrained from saying anything about the fact that more than a generation had passed since Vera Solane became internationally famous.

"Mother," she began hesitantly, changing the subject,

"tell me about Victor and Pat, will you? From what you've said, I'm sure your new husband is a good man, and I'm looking forward to meeting him tomorrow. But Pat . . . well, I don't think I like him very much. No, that's not accurate. I know I don't like him . . . why pretend?"

"Really, dear? Why on earth not? Victor and I felt that you two would hit it off very well."

"It's just that he seems to think he owns Foxdale. He was showing me around this morning so that I could see what progress has been made, and he kept saying, 'we'll do this' and 'we'll accomplish that.'" Caroline looked down at her hands in her lap, wondering how to phrase the next question. Finding no subtle way, she just plunged in. "You do still own Foxdale, don't you? You didn't sign it over in a marriage agreement or anything?"

"Why, Caroline, what a ridiculous notion! Of course I still own the estate! It's the only thing I have left, really. Besides it's all I have to leave to you when I die," Vera added. "Victor and I did have a legal agreement drawn up, but he was very sweet about Foxdale. He said that everyone must have something of his very own to cherish."

"Then why does Pat assume such an air of ownership?"

"Perhaps because he's worked so hard, dear. His uncle put him through school, and Pat has a degree in engineering, but his real love is wine. There's nothing that boy wants more than to be a successful vintner."

"Was there an arrangement, then, that Pat would restore the estate and in exchange be given control over the winery? You do know, don't you, that Pat intends to bottle blended wines?"

Vera daintily spread a curl of fresh butter onto her roll

and took a bite. "I'm not aware of any such arrangement, and Victor would never agree to anything concerning this estate without consulting me first." She smiled pleasantly, then sipped her coffee. "As for the actual winemaking, I know nothing about such things, dear. Is blending such a bad thing to do?"

Caroline shrugged her shoulders. "It's not illegal, if that's what you mean. But it does show a blatant disregard for fine wine, and a crassness that a dedicated vintner would disdain."

"Well, I'm sure Pat has his reasons, dear. You mustn't take everything to heart."

She was about to reply to her mother when the telephone interrupted them. Caroline watched her mother gracefully rise and pick up the receiver. "Hello?"

There was a silence while the other party spoke, and then Vera extended the phone to Caroline. "It's for you, darling. Dr. John Clarke, calling long-distance from England."

"Johnnie...." She rose to take the receiver, feeling both elated that he'd called and a little apprehensive that something might be wrong. She glanced over at her mother, but Vera had resumed reading the reviews, and Caroline was aware that the woman had reverted to her own private world.

Chapter 5

"Is everything all right?" she asked John immediately.

John's chuckle was reassuring. "That's just what I was going to ask you," he said. Then Caroline could hear him reprimanding the family dog, a huge Irish wolfhound. "Get down, Winston! You know you're not allowed on the couch. He misses you," he said to her. "He's been impossible since you left."

"Give him a hug for me," Caroline said, thinking fondly of the enormous lovable beast. "And you? How are you and the rest of the family?"

There was a crackle of static on the line for a few seconds, then John said, "I miss you, too. We all do, of course. Mother and the girls have gone off to Brighton for their annual holiday. So, since I was sitting here all alone, heating up some soup and a leftover chop and feeling terribly sorry for myself, I decided to telephone. How are things going so far?"

Caroline's eyes darted to her mother. "Oh, okay, I guess," she answered cautiously.

"You don't sound very enthusiastic, Caroline. Is she being absolutely rotten to you already?"

"No, no! Quite the reverse."

"Do I gather that you're not free to speak right now? Is someone in the room with you?"

Bless John's heart and his keen sensibilities. "Yes, as a matter of fact, mother's looking very well. I'd almost expected to find her sitting in a wheelchair covered with a lap robe, but she's as beautiful as ever."

Vera looked up and in a stage whisper said, "Fat chance of ever finding me in a wheelchair!"

Gesturing to silence her, Caroline asked, "Couldn't you get away for a vacation as well, Johnnie?"

"No, not right now anyway. There's some kind of new virus going around, and I think most of Hampstead has come down with it."

More loud crackling disrupted the line, and Caroline could barely hear John muttering something. "We seem to have a very bad connection, John," she said loudly.

"What?" he yelled over the irritating sound.

"A bad connection!" she said distinctly. "Get the operator to credit your call and place it again." Just as she said the last three words, the noise stopped.

"Look, let me call you back," John suggested in a normal voice. "This is maddening."

Caroline agreed and hung up, then she turned to Vera. "He's going to call back, mother. Is it all right if I take it in father's study? I mean, if it's not being used by Victor these days. That way I won't disturb you."

"Certainly, dear, though you're hardly disturbing me.

Victor does use that room himself, but I'm sure he wouldn't mind. However, a word of warning: he's fiercely private and wouldn't want anything on his desk touched."

Kissing her mother lightly on the cheek, Caroline dashed out of the room and ran back downstairs. The study was next to her bedroom, with only a linen closet separating the two rooms. She remembered that her father used to read far into the night in the study. He always left his door open in case Caroline should have a nightmare or need him for any reason. She smiled fondly at the memory, knowing that her father's concern had been totally unnecessary, since her governess had the room on the other side.

She paused only for a moment before entering the study, feeling a little apprehensive about opening the door to so many memories. But then the telephone rang dully through the door, and she rushed inside. One look told her that she needn't have worried about any painful memories. The room had been totally redecorated.

"Hello, Johnnie?"

"Yes, that's much better," he said. "Are you able to speak any more freely now?"

She nodded. "I've come downstairs," she answered. "I'm all alone now."

"Is it possible that your mother might be eavesdropping on the extension?"

"Oh Johnnie, I know you don't like her, but that's unfair. She's really very sweet and means well. Please don't spoil this call by being nasty about her."

"You're right," he said slowly. "I'm sorry. Maybe if I met her I might be able to understand a little better."

"I'm sure of it," Caroline said. "It's so great to hear your voice, John. It makes me feel as if you're just next door."

"And I feel as if you've been gone for months," he replied. "But truthfully, how is it going?"

"Okay. Mother and I had a tiff last night, but I don't think it'll happen again."

"Who won?" he asked, laughing. "Christians, zero; lions, ten?"

"No, nothing like that. But I do think we have a clearer understanding of each other now. She confessed that she'd remarried without telling me, and I became really annoyed."

"Can't blame you," he said genuinely. "What's the new husband like?"

"I don't know. I won't meet him till tomorrow, but I've met his nephew. If they're anything alike, I'll be home a lot sooner than I expected."

"Say that again."

"Say what, Johnnie?"

"Home—as if you meant it. This really is your home, you know." His voice was soft and low.

"That's dear of you, and I hope you all know how much I appreciate the way you've always treated me like one of the family."

John was quiet for a moment, then said, "So you don't like the nephew. What's he like?"

"Arrogant, overbearing, olympian...."

"Wait a second," John interrupted, laughing. "How did you decide all that in less than twenty-four hours?"

"It became quite obvious when I went for a walk with him this morning," she replied. "I'd say you and Pat are about the same age, give or take a year, but he has none of your dignity or gentle ways. He's pompous and conceited, and...."

"I see. And I suppose he's handsome," John prodded.

"Only if you like that type—all brawn and no brains. He's taken over the rebuilding of Foxdale without so much as a by-your-leave!"

"You mean your mother didn't agree?"

"Well, no," Caroline said, backing down. "Mother thinks it's all just wonderful, but she doesn't know what his plans are."

"Listen," John said, sounding hurried, "my three minutes are going to be up in a second. Why don't you write and tell me what's happening?"

"All right, I promise," she said. "And Johnnie? Thank you for calling."

"I, uh—"

"Yes, what is it?" She could almost envision John swallowing hard, the way he always did when he was uncomfortable about something.

"I just wanted you to know that I love you."

She smiled. "And I love you, too, John."

"That's not...never mind. I'll write to you, too. Take care of yourself, Caroline."

They said goodbye, and Caroline hung up the receiver, feeling a little uneasy. It had seemed as if John had wanted to say a great deal more but didn't know how. She leaned back in Victor's desk chair and looked around the ornately furnished room. It was the total antithesis of what it had once been. Whereas her father's tastes had run to overstuffed easychairs and sturdy functional tables and bookcases, this room now reflected elegant taste. Everything about it was inordinately neat and organized. Each article of furniture had been carefully arranged to show it to best advantage, and even the papers on Victor's desk were meticulously organized in Italian tooled-leather portfolios.

Again, Caroline was impressed with the paintings on the walls. As in the rest of the house, the majority of them were impressionist works. Then Caroline noticed a very familiar painting at the far corner of the study. Rising, she crossed over to examine it more carefully. It was Bruegel's *The Return of the Hunters*. It was a work that had been discussed at school for its remarkable simplicity in a century that emphasized the intricate and ornate. Sixteenth-century artists reveled in elaborate detail, and what made Pieter Bruegel's work distinctive was his ability to suggest, rather than render precisely.

Staring at the canvas, she admired the scope and power of the painting, the way the artist managed to convey the cold stillness of a winter scene. Like the Cézanne in the living room, it was a superb copy. Then Caroline remembered that Victor was an art dealer and would have access to the best copies available. Still, it was odd that a dealer would want a copy. She remembered a lecture at art school given by a visiting art dealer who had sneered at the notion of hanging a copy in his home. Most dealers, he had said, buy up the works of promising young artists in the hopes that they will one day be considered masters. Victor must have different ideas, she mused.

Then, thinking that she'd heard a light clicking sound behind her, she turned away from the painting. But there was nothing there except the floor-to-ceiling bookcase that lined the opposite wall. *That's funny*, she thought, *I could've sworn....* She dismissed the notion with a shrug and left the room quietly. Well, there was one thing she knew for sure: Victor and Pat couldn't be all that much alike. Her stepfather's taste in decor and art showed that he was a civilized and refined man.

As she walked toward her own room, Caroline suddenly realized that she'd never thought of Victor as her stepfather before. It felt strangely awkward to face the fact that she had a stepfather, especially one she'd never even met.

At dinner Pat sat at Vera's left, directly across from Caroline, who was terribly uncomfortable with the arrangement. Señora Mendez served their meal assisted by Consuelo, who seemed all thumbs whenever she was near Pat. With these tensions in the room, the entire meal would have been a disaster, if it weren't for Vera.

Vera had not seemed to notice how strained Caroline felt seated across from the young man, and she had maintained a stream of innocuous chatter.

She explained how Caroline had been born in New York instead of in London, where Vera had been singing. "There was simply no way for me to get back to London, given my tour schedule," she explained.

"But surely you weren't singing for your full term," Pat said, sipping his coffee.

Vera smiled whimsically. "Well, I certainly wasn't performing in an opera," she responded. "But I did have a series of concerts lined up. What people rarely understand is that a singer doesn't dare take any time away for herself. Not performing for a period of five or six months is terribly destructive. The public forgets you, impressarios become accustomed to working with others, and it can take forever to rebuild your status."

"I don't think I'd like that kind of a career," Pat said, his hazel eyes looking pale in the flickering candlelight. "I need my freedom too much, I suppose."

"*Por los gustos hicieron los colores*," Caroline said, with a slight edge to her voice.

"What's that, dear?"

"It's an old Spanish saying. Loosely translated, it means that the colors were invented to suit varied tastes."

"How interesting. But you see, Pat," Vera continued, "that's why Caroline was born in the States instead of England. She had her choice of citizenship until she was twenty-one...."

"And you chose England," Pat said, turning toward Caroline.

"I don't remember New York," she answered tersely, as if any fool should realize that. "Besides, except for this estate, England has been my home. It's been good to me, and it was my father's native country."

Pat shook his head. "It just seems that everyone wants to be an American these days—lower taxes, more opportunity, higher wages...."

"There are more important things in life than money," Caroline said flatly and pointedly, still irked by Pat's intention to blend the wines from their vineyard.

He laughed abruptly. "Name one."

"Love, honor, health, integrity, loyalty...shall I go on?"

"Well, yes, dear, those are very important things, to

be sure. But believe me, it's very difficult to maintain any of those virtues without money." Vera leaned toward Caroline as if to emphasize her next remarks. "I have never forgotten my childhood, dear.

"We were immigrants and dirt poor. My father worked on the docks, and my mother worked in a factory in the garment district. During the Depression, I had to wear secondhand clothes from charities. At the age of six, I had only one pair of shoes, and I had nothing else to put on my feet, even in the winter. It was humiliating, and I've never forgotten it," she concluded, the pain obvious in her face.

Caroline looked at her mother intently. "I never knew that you'd been that poor," she said slowly, seeing her mother in a new light.

Vera nodded. "I don't talk about it much, as I'm sure you can understand. The tenement we lived in was infested with roaches and rats—"

"Mother, how awful!" Caroline interrupted.

Vera smiled gently. "Yes, it was. And I vowed never to be poor when I grew up." Vera paused for a moment, then went on to talk about the Depression in more general terms.

"If you got sick, back then you went to bed and hoped it wouldn't kill you, because you couldn't afford a doctor. Clothes were mended over and over again, until the original pattern almost disappeared. People your age tend to think that the Depression only took place in 1929 because that's when the Crash hit. But it went on for years. So before you get all carried away with your lofty notions about what's important in life, Caroline, try to remember that not everyone has had your advantages."

Pat tilted his chair back, looking at Vera. "I have a new respect for you, Vera. I hadn't realized how hard you'd had to work to get to the top."

Vera smiled at him, then turned again to her daughter. "Perhaps now, Caroline, you have some idea why my career has always been the most important thing in my life. It wasn't because I didn't love you that I had to be away so much, or that I sent you to live with the Clarkes...."

Taken aback by this startling information, Caroline's mind was a jumble of confused thoughts. What her mother had revealed put an entirely new perspective on things, and Caroline needed some time to sort it all out. But she did regret her earlier barb at Pat in front of her mother; she must have sounded like a spoiled brat!

"Well, I'm off," Pat said, rising from his chair. "I can't keep the same hours the Spanish do," he added, grinning.

"Good night, Pat," Vera said. "Sleep well."

Caroline mumbled something and poured herself another cup of coffee. When Pat had left the dining room, she turned to her mother. "Tell me about Victor," she asked, trying to get the conversation into a more pleasant subject. "What's he like?"

Vera brightened visibly at her question. "Well, he's very persuasive," she said, laughing. "He cajoled me into marrying him, after all. And if he uses those same powers of persuasion on his clients, it's no wonder he's made a fortune as an art dealer."

"I've admired his taste in paintings," said Caroline. "I only hope he doesn't grill me about art. I'll never measure up to an art dealer in a discussion about the old masters."

She was just about to launch into a description of an exhibition of a talented young artist's works which she'd seen in a gallery in London before she left when she caught Vera staring off into space. Obviously Vera was about as interested in modern art as Caroline was in opera.

Caroline sensed, too, that her mother had not yet finished exorcising the demons of her past. Gently she asked, "Did you ever go back to your old neighborhood in Brooklyn?"

"Not often. When I was in New York, I'd send a car for my parents to be brought to the hotel where I was staying or send them tickets to hear me perform." Vera shrugged, a pained expression in her eyes. "It's difficult to explain, Caroline. I realize it makes me sound hard and calloused, but I'd come so far from my origins. . . . I was a different person, and I had nothing in common with those people anymore. My parents seemed to sense it, too, and were never comfortable around me."

"And your friends?"

"I saw some of them after my mother's funeral. My best friend was thirty and looked forty-five. She had seven children and was expecting another. She'd dropped out of high school and married the boy she'd been dating for two years." Vera shook her head sadly. "What a waste. A lovely, animated young girl turned into an old woman, stuck with a life she couldn't understand."

"Maybe not, mother. Maybe she was happy, despite her poverty," Caroline said.

"Happy people do not get old before their time, Caroline. They also don't have pinched mouths and whining voices. No, dear, you simply don't know what you're talking about. Most of us make our own lives," Vera said, her tone becoming hard, "and if you're willing to settle for what you've got, that's all you'll ever have. Most people don't know how to fight back, and that's the simple truth of it."

"But," Caroline said softly, "look at the price you've had to pay for fighting back."

Vera's eyebrows rose quizzically. "Price?"

"Yes. You were seldom with the man you loved, and you never knew your own daughter." She said it quietly, without rancor. After hearing about her childhood, Caroline felt a little sorry for her mother.

The woman's expression became enigmatic. "There's a price for everything, my dear. Your father was a good man, sincere and devoted, and I loved him deeply. But he had no ambition. I knew that, and I didn't care because I loved him. But it only intensified my own drive for success." Then her voice hardened again. "Had I abandoned my career to be with the two of you, we'd have been struggling to put food on the table. Besides, don't forget that I love my work . . . or did, I should say."

Caroline toyed with her cup, trying to absorb all the things her mother had revealed this evening. Finally, putting her napkin on the table, she said, "I'd like to go for a walk. Would you care to join me?"

"No, thank you, dear. You go ahead. I think I'll go to bed early."

Rising, Caroline walked to the double doors then paused. "Mother were you happy to have a baby when I was born? Was I a wanted child?" She could see Vera's back stiffen slightly.

"You and I made a pact to be truthful," the woman's low voice began. "No, Caroline, I didn't want a child then. Perhaps never. I knew I couldn't be a good mother."

"Then why . . . ?"

"Because it was your father's most ardent wish. You were born to keep him company."

Caroline could feel the tears gathering in her eyes, and though she was grateful to her mother for being honest, the truth hurt deeply nonetheless. Wordlessly, Caroline went through the vast tiled foyer and outside into the cool night air.

Chapter 6

It was chilly enough to require a sweater, but Caroline didn't feel like going back into the house at that moment. She felt disoriented and terribly sad, as well as emotionally drained. Her first two days with her mother had been a strain. Then there had been Pat O'Flaherty to contend with and his take-charge attitude about the villa. And his impertinence in kissing her! Added to all that were her mother's admissions at dinner.

Earlier that day she'd started a letter to John. She'd just finished the first page when she became aware that the house had fallen strangely quiet. Then she realized that it was *siesta* time. It was going to take her a while to reaccustom herself to the Spanish way of life, she wrote to John. While she liked having her main meal at midday, she had always felt that *siesta* was more of a nuisance than anything else. Shops were closed, people disappeared, business stopped—virtually the whole of Spain took a nap from two until four o'clock. Then they went back to work until eight. Supper wasn't usually eaten until around nine or ten o'clock at night, yet everyone was expected to be up and ready for work by eight the next morning.

Caroline's thoughts returned to the letter, and she wondered how she could explain to John her confused emotions at hearing her mother's story. She knew it would be useless to try to tell him until she could sort things out more for herself. While she could now appreciate her mother's driving need to have a successful career, Caroline still could not sympathize with her mother's decision. In essence, her mother had given up her life in the pursuit of fame. Yet, what did she have to show for those long hard years? A scrapbook and a marriage of convenience? Despite everything—the adulation of the public, the parties, and the celebrities she'd met— all her mother really had now was her memories.

While Vera had said that Victor adored her, what good was that if her mother couldn't return the feeling? Didn't it make her feel guilty to know that she couldn't love him in the same way? Obviously not.

Caroline couldn't understand it. Had Vera's ego become so inflated that she actually believed she was doing Victor a favor by marrying him? And what kind of man was Victor O'Flaherty for accepting those terms. Being wealthy, he could have had his pick of any woman he wanted. Why would he choose someone who didn't return his love?

Caroline stopped walking and sat on a garden bench. Perhaps she wasn't being fair. She was sure that her mother did love Victor . . . in her own way. But she was also sure that it was a love without passion. Could it be that Vera and Victor were too old to be concerned with romantic love? That was inconceivable to Caroline.

There were many things she knew she didn't understand, but she knew one thing for certain: Vera's marriage to Victor made far more sense than his interest in Vera. Wouldn't it be demeaning to love someone desperately and know that it wasn't returned?

Yes, she could understand Vera a little better now. She had created her own world of illusions and perfections to shut out her hard and humiliating origins. Her mother simply wanted everything to be beautiful and exciting, and financial security was one way to insure that she got what she wanted. She was even willing to pass up a chance at real love, to settle for something less. It seemed to Caroline a very empty way to lead one's life.

Questions flooded her mind as she rose restlessly from the bench and continued walking. Didn't her mother have moments of loneliness, perhaps even sadness? Could she confide these to Victor, or did she have to keep them bottled up inside?

Caroline just didn't know what to think. She stooped to wrench a weed out from between two flagstones, and the thought she'd been trying to avoid surfaced of its own will. If she had been born simply to keep her father company, why did Vera want to know her now? Had Caroline just become another facet of her mother's vision of perfection? Was Vera just acting out the role of the contrite mother?

She wished John were there so she could discuss all this with him. As it was, she had said very little about her own feelings in her letter to him. Instead, what she'd written so far resembled a travelogue, with details of what Foxdale was like and a searing paragraph on Pat...omitting his kiss, though she didn't know why.

As she turned a corner in the garden path, the tall hedges partially obscured the moonlight, and Caroline had to pay more attention to where she was going. Though this section seemed to have been tended recently, she didn't want to risk missing a step and falling in the dark.

Feeling cold and still very confused, Caroline stopped once again. The fragrance of roses told her where she was in relation to the house—the rose garden had always been her father's favorite place. At the thought of her father she realized that, despite all her mother's protestations to the contrary, there wasn't any way that she could believe her mother had loved her all those years. She'd wanted to; she'd hoped to...but it was impossible. Caroline knew what the love of a parent was like. Although she'd secretly harbored a wish that Vera had yearned to be with her husband and baby, Caroline knew it just wasn't true. Vera had done Elliot Mesner a favor by having a child; she might as well have gone out and bought him a dog. It hadn't been circumstances that had kept her away; it had been Vera's own compulsions. Though Caroline could now understand the reasons for her rejection a little better, it didn't lessen the pain, even after all these years.

Suddenly the stone beneath Caroline's feet began to vibrate slightly. Her problems were immediately left behind as terror swept through her. Was it an earthquake? Then she realized that she'd never heard of an earthquake in the vicinity. Curious, she took a step backward. The minor, almost rhythmic shuddering continued, and she bent down to touch the flagstone.

"Did you lose an earring?"

Caroline gasped in fright, then found herself looking up at Pat O'Flaherty. "Do you always sneak up on people like that?" she asked angrily.

He laughed. "I didn't. I was just taking a short walk before turning in, and I find you in the dark, on your hands and knees."

Caroline straightened up. "I was trying to figure out what could be causing the vibrations beneath my feet."

"Vibrations!" Pat repeated. "What are you talking about?"

"Right here. I could feel them...but...they seem to have stopped now."

"Yes, and the zebras have gone to bed, and the elves are in the trees mending our shoes."

She didn't even deign to reply to his sarcasm.

"Well, come on, Caroline. It is a bit much, don't you think? Why on earth would the ground vibrate? It's as solid here as the Rock of Gibraltar."

"You're infuriating," she said, attempting to walk past him back to the house. "I simply commented on a strange sensation and you're treating me as if I were a child."

"I don't know what it is you have against me, Caroline," Pat answered, catching her arm with his hand, "but it's becoming annoying. I've never done anything to you, nor is it likely I ever would. But you act as if I'm destroying this estate instead of rebuilding it. Are you afraid my fee will be too high, that I'll bankrupt your mother? Because if that's it, you needn't worry. As

I told you this morning, Victor's paying for everything."

"Let go of me, Pat," she said slowly, seething.

"No good-night kiss?" he teased, pulling her to him.

"Are you always so rude?"

"Only with the prettier ones," he answered. Then he released her. "There's many a lass who'd welcome my advances," he said playfully, his Irish brogue in evidence.

"Then go spend your time with them!" Furious, Caroline made her way back to the house.

Lying in bed a little while later, her anger abating, Caroline thought back to the vibrations she had felt near the rosebushes. It had felt as if a subway had been barreling by on tracks, just below the stone slabs. What could have caused such tremors? Obviously, she couldn't ask Pat, even though he was an engineer.... Pat. Her anger returned with renewed force as she thought about how sarcastic he'd been when she'd told him about the vibrations. He'd just laughed at her...didn't even honor her with a civil reply!

When, at length, Caroline finally succumbed to sleep, her last thoughts were on rising early to return to the roses and find out a little more about those mysterious vibrations....

SHORTLY AFTER BREAKFAST, Caroline and Vera went into the living room to await Victor's arrival from the airport. "He's very punctual," Vera said, smoothing out the skirt of her beautiful silk dress.

Within half an hour, the sound of the sedan's tires on the gravel drive reached them, and moments later Victor O'Flaherty came into the room. His hair, once brown, was now graying at the temples, and the lines on his tanned, lean face suggested that he might be about fifty years old. He was of medium build and dressed with the quiet elegance that Caroline would have expected of a wealthy, yet tasteful art dealer.

He came into the living room and kissed Vera on the cheek then turned to be introduced to Caroline. "We're both so glad you decided to accept the invitation," he began, smiling broadly. "I'm looking forward to getting to know you, Caroline."

"Thank you," she said simply, not quite certain of what she should do. "It was kind of you to ask me," she added, trying to sound warm and cordial.

In temperament, Victor wasn't at all what she'd expected. Somehow, she'd pictured the sort of person who'd wring his hands a great deal in his anxiety to please. She hadn't thought of her mother's second husband as this very self-possessed, dignified man.

"I've brought you a present, darling," Victor said, turning and putting his arm around Vera's shoulder. Then he moved back into the front hall, returning with a parcel that had to be a painting. "Remember when we were in Milan, and you admired that young artist whose work was in the gallery?" As he spoke, he removed the brown wrapping paper. "Well, I managed to strike a deal for it this trip."

"Oh Victor! How wonderful! Look, Caroline, isn't it the most lovely thing you've ever seen?"

Caroline stepped forward to get a closer look at the small painting. The background was deep rich brown and almost sensual in the way it set off the red velvet drapes that framed the central figure. It was the profile of a woman leaning forward as though to inhale the fragrance of a single rose.

Though Caroline could appreciate that the painting was very well done, and even possessed a kind of charm, she felt the arrangement of the various components in the picture left a great deal to be desired. She was surprised that Victor, a knowledgeable art connoisseur, would purchase such a work, but then she realized it had been bought to please Vera, whose tastes in art were far from sophisticated.

"It's lovely," she agreed, smiling politely.

"It's called *The Rose Lady*," Vera said, taking the picture over to the windows for better light. Frowning for a second, she turned to her husband, saying, "Now, this isn't a copy, is it?"

He smiled. "No, dear, it's the real thing."

Trying to make conversation, Caroline said, "You know, that Cézanne on the far wall would've fooled me anytime." She paused uncertainly.

"Oh?" Victor raised his eyebrows, waiting for her to continue.

"Mother told me that you're a dealer, and that all the works in this house are copies."

"That's correct. Are you interested in art, Caroline?"

"Yes, I am. Actually, I'm an art student."

A strange expression flickered across Victor's face, almost as if he were momentarily angry. But the look was gone in a split second, and his gracious smile returned. Crossing over to where Vera had seated herself, he answered, "I wish I'd known. I could have been looking forward to having a great deal to talk about with my stepdaughter."

Caroline smiled. "Well, hardly. I've studied the masters, but my primary interest is commercial art. I don't think I'd be able to hold my own in a discussion of the great works of art in general."

"Don't be so self-effacing, my dear. You knew that was a Cézanne at once, I'm sure."

"Oh, yes, and I noticed the superb Bruegel in the den." For some reason, Caroline wished she hadn't mentioned being in Victor's den, but it was too late. But if the information had shocked or offended Victor, he didn't let it show.

He pulled a panatela from a sterling-silver cigarette case in his inside pocket, lighting it slowly and savoring it. "Where's Pat?" he asked casually.

Vera placed the painting on a long table near the windows. "He should be along any moment," she answered.

As if on cue, the ruggedly handsome young man strode into the room. "Sorry to be late," he said, smiling boyishly and obviously delighted to see his uncle. "I noticed this morning that one of the retaining walls near the sheds was beginning to come loose. It took longer to fix than I expected."

"That's quite all right, my boy," Victor said, extending his right hand. "I'm just glad you were able to repair it before any damage was done."

Pat grinned fraternally. "You're looking well, Victor. Have a good trip?"

"Actually, far better than I'd anticipated." He turned, puffing on his thin cigar. "As a matter of fact, dear, how would you like to go to California this fall?"

Vera was delighted. "I'd love it! I haven't been there since...oh, ages ago. Which part?"

"Southern. I've some clients interested in a few oils and watercolors. Bel Air and Beverly Hills area. But we could fly up to San Francisco afterward, if you like."

"I do wish you wouldn't work so hard, Victor," Vera said with a resigned sigh. "You're supposed to be retired, after all."

Victor winked at Caroline. "Don't listen to those doctors, Vera. They're all a bunch of worried old ladies."

"I wish that were true," she answered, obviously thinking of her own career. Then she brightened, saying, "But I do understand, Victor. Your work is your world."

"Not quite," he replied, looking at her lovingly. "You are."

Though it was a gracious thing to say, Caroline found herself a little surprised by Victor's expression. Though he was smiling at Vera devotedly, Caroline sensed that he was playing some kind of a game. It was as if he knew the right things to say, and the appropriate accompanying gestures, but he didn't really mean it. It was a strange reaction for her to have, and she soon put it down to an overactive imagination. Vera herself said how much he adored her, and his concern and attentiveness certainly seemed to support her claim.

"Will lunch be served on time?" Victor asked, seating himself next to Vera on the velvet settee.

"Of course, dear. It always is when you're home."

"Then, Patrick, since it's Sunday, why don't you fix us each a Bloody Mary to celebrate my return and Caroline's first Sunday with us."

"Certainly, Victor."

Out of the corner of her eye, Caroline watched Pat as he deftly took the various ingredients he needed from the bottom shelf of the service cart. He moved athletically, with the easy masculine grace that she had come to associate with him.

"...so I thought the two of you might enjoy it."

Caroline suddenly realized that Victor had been speaking to her. Flushing, she said, "I'm sorry, my mind was wandering. What did you say?"

He nodded at her as if to say he understood. "The *sardanas*," he said. "I was suggesting that Pat take you down to Badalona this evening after dinner. I'm sure you'd enjoy watching the dances after such a long time."

As he spoke, she watched Pat carrying a tray with four drinks toward her mother. He winked at Caroline as he crossed in front of her, and she knew she was trapped. Whether she liked it or not, Pat was going to be her escort. "Why don't we all go?" she suggested enthusiastically.

"No, no. I'd prefer to spend this evening alone with Vera," Victor said, putting her arm through his. "I haven't seen her in a week! Besides, young people shouldn't be saddled with tag-along oldsters," he added, laughing.

"Hardly, Victor," Vera interjected. "I can still kick as high as ever and probably higher than my own daughter!"

"It would be my pleasure," Pat said, bending to serve a drink to Caroline who was seated on a couch. "I haven't been down to the *cantina* in weeks, and it would give us a chance to get to know each other better."

She took the dark red drink and glowered at Pat,

knowing that the others couldn't see her expression. He knew perfectly well that there was no way out of Victor's suggestion. All she could do was agree, with as much grace as she could muster.

"Then it's settled," Victor said.

Chapter 7

In Catalan, the most northeastern province of Spain, the Sunday *sardanas* were an ancient tradition. In twos and threes, the villagers of Badalona would take their evening constitutional along the broad avenue that faced the Mediterranean, nodding to acquaintances and pausing occasionally to talk to friends. Caroline remembered these evenings fondly, recalling how her father used to bring her to the shore to enjoy the cool evening, the music and the dancing.

It was nearly ten o'clock when Patrick pulled his jeep over to the curb and helped her down. No cars were permitted beyond that point, and they would have to walk the short distance to the cobblestoned promenade. On one side of the street was the sea, dazzling in the setting sun; on the other were a profusion of small simple restaurants, rather rundown hotels and a couple of bars. The *cantinas* were very homey places, run by the local people as gathering places, rather than pretentious seafront bars. In all the times Caroline had been there as a girl, she could not remember seeing anyone rowdy or drunk, except the occasional tourist.

As they approached she could see that most of the outdoor tables were already occupied. The familiar strains of violins being tuned to flutes, coupled with strumming guitars, made her pulse quicken with excitement.

"Hey, cheer up," Pat said. "You haven't said a word since we left the house. Let's pretend we've just met and have a good time, okay?"

She was entirely too elated to resist his suggestion of a truce. Happily, she nodded at him. "Let's find a table quickly, or it'll be too late," she said.

Pat grinned, and taking her by the hand, led her through the throngs of people gathering to listen to the music. "Here, this looks all right," he said. "The best dancers always come to this *cantina*, and you'll get a good view of them from here."

A waiter came toward them shaking his head and speaking rapidly in Spanish. "What's he saying?" Pat asked.

"Another couple are seated here," she translated. Then looking back at the waiter, she asked him something in Spanish.

The watier beamed, obviously delighted that she spoke Spanish.

Turning to Pat in anticipation of his question she explained, "I asked if we couldn't share the table, and he's going to explain it to the other couple. He says we should go ahead and take our seats."

"That's very nice of him," Pat said, digging into his pocket.

Caroline put her hand on his arm. "Don't tip him, Pat. He'd be offended."

He looked at her curiously. "But I always tip when I come down here."

"The Catalonians are very proud, Pat. You tip for a service, but never for a favor...unless it's something really out of the ordinary. He'd far prefer it if you thanked him genuinely. Later, if you'd like leave him a larger tip than usual for whatever services he provides."

"I guess they've had me pegged as a tourist the other times I've been here," he replied, pulling the chair back for Caroline.

"They never used to dislike tourists, and I doubt they do now. It's just that they resent foreigners thinking that people have to be bought. They consider it rude."

Suddenly the music started up in earnest, and Caroline couldn't resist glancing at Pat with an expectant smile. The *sardanas* were very much like Greek music, their tempo slow, yet provocative. She loved the feeling of being out in the night air, smelling the salt from the sea across the street and listening to the haunting melodies.

Soon people began to dance, moving slowly into groups that broke up to form circles within circles. With their arms about one another's shoulders, they began to sway and dip in tune to the rhythm.

Their waiter came back, bending low so that he could hear their order. "*Vino, tinto,*" Pat said quietly.

Caroline had to smile. "You learned that quickly enough," she teased.

"Shh," he said seriously. "Listen to the music."

Returning her attention to the dancers, Caroline began to relax for the first time since returning to Spain. It was such a pleasure to be back again, among people who lived simply and didn't need very much to be contented. A good crop, a good haul from the sea, health and sunshine, a little wine, music. . .how vastly different from her mother's world or even from the life she'd led in London. Good friends, a boyfriend, a shared experience at the end of the week's hard work—these were things Caroline could appreciate.

During the applause that followed the first dance, Pat leaned toward her. "I didn't think you could look happy," he said, his hazel eyes probing hers.

"I guess I've been finding the past few days rather a strain," Caroline admitted ruefully. "But I'm finding this evening delightful. I feel comfortable in this happy, simple town."

"Now we have something in common," Pat said, laughing. "Mind you, I think Victor's one of the most terrific fellows in the world, but I'd never be able to live like he does. I hate wearing a tie, and I wouldn't know one designer from another. I can't stand parties and idle chitchat, either."

Perhaps because of the wine—though she doubted it—Caroline found herself liking Pat O'Flaherty as the evening wore on. His strutting, overbearing manner was nowhere in evidence, and she realized that he was really a very serious, sincere young man. Caroline heard about his student days in Dublin, when he was learning to be an engineer. Throughout that time, he explained, he was yearning to come to Spain, to live and work outdoors and use his hands to build a future. He told her of his introduction to fine wines and how he decided to become a vintner himself one day.

Caroline had been tempted to ask him how he could have such high aspirations and yet be willing to blend the wines of Foxdale, but she realized the time wasn't right. Perhaps her mother had been right; maybe Pat did have his reasons, and in time she might understand them.

"You have no other family, Pat? Just Victor?"

"Just Victor," he replied. "Without him, I'd be nothing more than a shanty Irishman, probably working in a coal mine like my father did. My parents were killed in a bus accident when I was just a little tyke, and Victor took me in."

She sat back, a mellow feeling slipping over her. "It's strange, isn't it, that Victor never married before. You'd think with a small child to care for, he would have wanted to have a wife to help him."

Pat grinned. "Actually, Victor doesn't like children. I didn't see that much of him when I was a child. He always packed me off to one school or another. But as I grew older and could be more of a companion to him, we became friends."

"You were born to keep him company." Vera's remark the night before sprang to Caroline's mind. In a way, she and Pat had quite a lot in common.

"It's midnight," he said unexpectedly, looking at his watch. "I hate to leave, but I've got to be up early tomorrow morning."

He looked so disappointed that Caroline said quickly, "Don't worry, Pat, there'll be other Sundays."

"Would you be meanin' that Miss Mesner, ma'am," he asked, exaggerating his brogue. "You'd not be teasin' a country lad?"

"Come on," she answered, laughing. "Let's go home."

Pat went inside to pay their bill, and she began to stroll toward the street. He joined her a couple of minutes later, and soon they were driving back up the winding road to Foxdale. It had been a wonderful evening, and Caroline was glad that she hadn't refused earlier.

He escorted her to the front door, quietly and almost bashfully.

"Aren't you coming in?" Caroline inquired.

"I live in the new wing, closer to the vineyards," he replied. "I'll leave you here, then go around from the outside. It'll disturb fewer people that way."

The moon was directly overhead, turning his black hair to silver in its light. "Then, good night, Pat. And thank you for a lovely time."

"Caroline," he said, rolling the "r" softly. "I haven't been much of a gentleman up until now, but I'd very much like to kiss you, if I may."

A little shyly, she took a step toward him. Pat's arms encircled her small waist, and he softly pressed his lips against hers. He held her gently, as if she might break, but his breath was coming rapidly. Moments later he broke away and said, "I'd best let you go before I forget myself. Good night, Caroline."

Pat began to walk quickly down the path toward the other wing. He paused just before he turned around the side of the house and, with a tilt of his head and a wave, he disappeared.

Caroline had to smile. That conceited Irishman knew perfectly well that she'd still be standing there watching him leave, but she was entirely too happy to care. Slowly, she opened the door and let herself into the house.

"I'm so glad you're home!"

She was completely unprepared to see Victor standing in the archway to the living room.

"What's wrong? What's happened?" she asked, suddenly tense.

He looked strained and disheveled, as if he'd been pacing for hours. "I'm not sure," he replied. "We were having supper, and Vera said she felt a little nauseous. I suggested a brandy to settle her stomach, and then about a half hour later, she turned as white as chalk and doubled up with stomach cramps."

"Where's mother now?"

"Upstairs, with the doctor," Victor answered. "I called him immediately, but we didn't know where to reach you and Pat."

"Pat should be in his room by now," Caroline said, worried about Vera. "I'll go upstairs, Victor. Why don't you ask Patrick to keep you company?"

Victor placed a cool dry hand on her arm. "Caroline, you don't know me very well yet, so what I'm going to say may sound melodramatic. But I want you to believe that I wouldn't want anything to happen to your mother. She means everything to me!"

"Of course, Victor. I didn't doubt that.... Do you think she's very ill?"

"I'm not sure," he replied hesitantly. He stared at her intently for a second, then as if struggling to keep a grip on himself, he turned and entered the living room.

For the second time that day Caroline had the distinct impression that Victor was acting out a part. But she was entirely too upset about Vera to dwell on it at that moment. . . .

THE PHYSICIAN HAD snow-white hair and suffered from arthritis in his hands. Caroline watched him administer an injection and marveled that he could manage the simple task at all. He rested his palm on Vera's forehead then turned to Caroline. "*La señora*, she will be better now, maybe sleep."

Caroline explained that she spoke a little Spanish and asked the doctor if he could diagnose what was wrong. With several philosophical shrugs and his head bobbing, he admitted that he didn't know. He'd taken a blood sample and would have it analyzed in the morning. Perhaps then they would know more.

She walked him to the bedroom door, explaining that Victor was downstairs and would show him out. Then she returned to her mother's bedside. "How're you feeling," she asked in a whisper.

"Sick!" The voice was a little weak, but the tone was angry.

"I know that, mother. Whatever the doctor gave you will probably take a little while before you'll feel its effects. Do you have any idea of what happened?"

Vera shook her hand weakly. "No. I was fine one moment, then sick the next."

"Could it be connected to your illness?"

"What illness?" Vera asked, her dark eyes dulled with medication.

Caroline wondered if the drug was dimming her mother's memory. "The one that caused you to retire, mother."

Slowly, as if with great effort, Vera lifted her hand from the bed and dismissed the question. "I had what amounts to varicose veins of the throat, Caroline. Somehow I don't think there's a connection between my throat and my stomach."

"I've never heard of such a thing," Caroline said, blinking in amazement.

"If you were a singer, you'd have heard about it. The strain on the vocal chords can prove too great, resulting in varicose veins." She sighed and leaned her head against the pillow drowsily. "It's a painful thing to have and unpleasant to talk about. Let's just say, I'm glad the whole thing is over."

"Oh, mother, it must have been horrible for you," Caroline cried sympathetically.

Vera smiled feebly. "To put it mildly," she agreed. "But it's cured now."

"Then why did you have to retire?"

"Because, dear," Vera began, "I would have had to have rested my vocal chords for more than a year. As it was, I wasn't permitted to speak for months. I had to carry a pad and pencil with me everywhere. The only way to regain my voice would have been to start all over again, to retrain my chords to their former control. That would take years, and at fifty," Vera concluded with a shrug, "there was no point."

Caroline shook her head. "You're truly an amazing woman, mother. It really hasn't been easy for you, has it?" she asked.

Her mother snorted silently. "Nothing's easy in this life, dear. You only hope and pray that after all your hard work, maybe you'll find a little joy. It's funny,"

Vera said, gesturing to Caroline to take the chair near the bed, "you know what my father used to say? He said that in order to survive in this world, you needed a strong stomach and a good sense of humor."

Caroline said nothing. Try as she did, she found it difficult to believe that this glamorous woman had ever known a day of deprivation, even when she was ill. Caroline tried to imagine Vera as a young girl in Brooklyn, living in squalor, but her mind couldn't picture it. What did strike her, however, was that her own life had probably been far better than most.

She couldn't remember ever having felt defeated, frustrated in hopes and ambitions, and it certainly wouldn't occur to her to ever think about having to "survive" the way her mother meant it. There was a vast difference between having hopes of success and having to struggle to stay alive. Caroline might have had an unusual childhood, but she'd always taken it for granted that there would be food on the table, that she'd have new shoes if she needed them, and that her world would be filled with kind people. How different her childhood was from Vera's origins!

"Ahh!" Vera rolled over and clutched her stomach.

"Can I get you something?" Caroline asked quickly, sitting forward in alarm.

"Get me a doctor, Caroline. A *real* doctor!"

"But the physician just left. . . ."

Although grimacing, Vera clearly was trying to make herself relax. She propped herself up, leaning back on her elbows, and shook her head. "He's an old man— used to cows and horses! Sometimes Victor hasn't got the brains of a gnat, bless him. Caroline," she said, turning her large pleading eyes toward her daughter, "get me a young, English-speaking doctor . . . please!"

"In Badalona?" Caroline's mind was racing. "John!" she said suddenly.

"I don't care what his name is, just get him!"

"You don't understand, mother. John Clarke . . . I could phone him, ask him to fly here first thing in the morning."

"Is he any good?"

Caroline had to smile. "Yes, he's an excellent physician. I'm just not sure if he can afford the fare right now. He's only just begun his practice."

Vera nodded sagely. "Oh, Victor will pay for his ticket, don't worry. Besides, if your John can claim to have Vera Solane as his patient, he'll have to turn away others."

"I'll telephone him right now," Caroline said, knowing perfectly well that John would never mention Vera's name to profit from it. It was interesting, though, that her mother automatically assumed that people would capitalize on an association with her, no matter how remote.

She rose, patting her mother's shoulder. "I won't be long."

"Use the phone in the sitting room," Vera said, "and, please, come right back!"

"All right, mother, don't get upset," Caroline agreed soothingly, on her way out. Then she stopped. "Shouldn't I ask Victor about the cost of airfare first?"

"Don't worry about it," Vera said, adding, "he'll do anything I ask."

Caroline was strangely disturbed by her mother's easy

confidence in her control over Victor. It didn't mesh with *her* view of Victor, who seemed so remote and untouchable. Not stopping to consider it any longer, Caroline went to the next room and picked up the telephone. She started when she realized that the phone was in use and would have put the receiver down at once had she not heard the tense strained tone of Victor's voice.

"No! Not here! I've told you that time and time again. My wife isn't to be disturbed for any reason, can't you understand?"

A rasping, uneducated voice replied: "Business is business, Mr. O'Flaherty. Any broad should understand that."

Victor's voice nearly hissed with fury. "My wife is not a 'broad,' and you're never to use that expression again. She's a treasure, more priceless than any work of art. She's not only the greatest contralto in the world, but she's alive and she's mine."

"Hey, okay! Don't get mad, Mr. O'Flaherty. I just thought it would save us both some time if I drove there so we could settle the details of our next deal."

"It won't be necessary." Victor answered levelly. "I'll prepare the information and send Alejandro over with it in the morning." He hung up abruptly.

Feeling a little guilty about overhearing even that much of the conversation, Caroline nonetheless wondered why on earth Victor would have any business connection with someone like that. The man's rough accent and vocabulary made Caroline doubt that he was part of the art world. . . . In any case, he was certainly not in Victor's league.

Perhaps the man is just a courier, arranging to pick up

some paintings, she thought. But why would Victor be handling trucking matters? Whatever the connection, the man couldn't be too far away from Badalona.

Although she sensed that things were not all that they appeared to be, Caroline forced herself to put her questions out of her mind until after she had reached John.

Chapter 8

Despite the late hour, John grasped the situation in a moment and started to ask Caroline cogent questions about how her mother's illness had started. She answered him as best she could, but not being present at the time of the initial attack, she'd been unable to give him any particulars—only what Victor had told her.

"Brandy was the worst thing in the world to give her," John said.

"Victor's not a doctor, John. He wouldn't know that."

"If it were up to me," he said irritably, "no one would be able to graduate from school without paramedic training. Oh well, too late now. What does the Spanish doctor think?"

She shrugged as she spoke. "He doesn't know, but he took a blood sample and will have it analyzed at the lab in the morning. Won't you come, Johnnie? Please? I'd feel so much better knowing mother is getting competent help."

"I'm sure the local doctor is a qualified man," John replied a little testily.

"He's very old, John, I'm not so sure. Anyway, the fact that he doesn't speak English is only irritating mother and making her worse. Besides," she said hesitantly, "I all but promised her you'd come."

"You shouldn't have done that, Caroline. I told you just this morning that Hampstead has a virus going around, and I'm needed right here. Just because you're mother's famous and—"

"That's not it, and you know it," she said. "It's because she *is* my mother, and she's afraid, and you're the best doctor I could think of."

John was silent for a few seconds, as if considering the situation, then he said, "I'll see if I can get Bosley to take over my patients for a day. But I really can't be gone more than twenty-four hours, Caroline. I'll come, but just because I don't want you worrying needlessly. It's probably nothing more than a touch of food poisoning anyway."

"Perhaps, John, but as you know, when you're sick and in pain you tend to imagine the worst," Caroline replied in defense of her mother.

"Yes, I know," he said, his manner more like his usual self. "All right, I'll phone the airlines now and see what flight I can get on. The moment I have any information, I'll call you back and let you know."

"Thank you, Johnnie, I know mother will appreciate it, and I certainly do."

She had no sooner hung up than Victor entered the sitting room quietly, his lean face looking worried and upset. "Is she sleeping?"

"I'm not sure," Caroline replied. "I've been on the phone, long-distance, to an English doctor I know."

His blue eyes narrowed as he looked at her carefully. "Why have you called in another doctor?" he asked.

"Because mother begged me to," she replied simply. "John's going to phone me back and let me know what flight he'll be on." She'd been about to ask if it had been all right to volunteer to pay John's fare but decided against it. She would rather let her mother handle it, rather than seem presumptuous.

Victor smiled ruefully, rubbing his temples with his thin fingers as he took a seat opposite her. "I suppose she's right," he said after a moment. "This isn't exactly a major city, and who knows how good that doctor is. I'm sure there must be excellent doctors in Barcelona who speak English, but your mother will be happier with an Englishman."

"I'll look in on her, Victor, just to make sure she's all right," Caroline said, rising and crossing the sitting room.

When she entered the bedroom, Caroline saw that Vera had dozed off. For the first time, she thought, she was seeing her mother totally defenseless. She looked tired, and despite the facelifts, Vera seemed to show her age in repose. Now that the sparkling eyes were closed, her mother's face seemed drawn and unhappy. She was still beautiful, but Caroline now thought there was something a little pathetic in her expression.

The ringing of the phone startled Caroline and she quickly pulled the door nearly closed as she returned to answer it. "Yes, John," she said, without any preliminaries.

"I'm booked on a British Airways flight arriving in Barcelona at nine-thirty in the morning. Can you meet me?"

"If I can borrow a car," she said, looking at Victor who nodded his consent. "Yes, it's all right." Swiftly, she jotted down the flight number, thanked John again and said good-night.

She and Victor remained silent for a while afterward, and Caroline could only dimly hear the rustling of the trees outside. It was a strange moment, seated there with a man she hardly knew who was her stepfather, with her mother, also a stranger, sick and afraid in the next room. Caroline sensed that each of them needed her for something: Victor, to console him; Vera to ease her fears.

Almost as if in a dream, Caroline became aware of the soft ticking of the clock on the corner of the mantel. It was a little past one in the morning. The house was totally quiet, and she realized then that Victor obviously had decided not to bother Patrick. In the stillness, it wouldn't have taken very much to make Caroline believe that she and Victor were the only two people still alive in the entire world. The eerie stillness sent a brief shiver through her.

"Cold?" Victor asked. "Shall I get you one of your mother's sweaters?"

"No, thank you," she said, smiling into the ice-blue eyes set in his lean tanned face. In his own way, he was a handsome man, Caroline thought; a little too effete for her own taste, but cosmopolitan and debonair.

"I adore her, you know," Victor said softly, out of the blue. "I've been a fanatic about fine art most of my life, Caroline—almost as dedicated as your mother has been to opera. But when I met Vera, something extraordinary happened."

Caroline nodded, encouraging him to continue. Obviously Victor wanted to talk, to confide in her...or perhaps he simply wanted her to come to know him and understand him.

"It's difficult to explain, actually," he said quietly. "I'd never wanted the obligations of marriage before meeting Vera. I traveled a great deal, went wherever I wanted to, whenever I wanted, and I never had to give a thought to what someone else might like to do. Hardly the sort any woman would want to marry. But two years ago I went to hear your mother in *Samson et Dalila* in Paris. I sat in my box mesmerized, like a little boy seeing his first electric train. She was not only beautiful, but her voice was like honey. Vera Solane, I thought, is a living work of art."

Victor rose and crossed over to the windows overlooking the rooftops of Badalona and the blanket of uninterrupted darkness beyond. "I don't know how you feel about art, Caroline," he continued. "Art has always been an intensely emotional experience for me. What my eyes perceive reaches into my soul and fills me with awe and respect. I experience an almost physical response to the beauty before me. But a painting is, after all, just an object to be looked at—perhaps touched—but unresponsive to human emotions. Perhaps that's why I'm a rather insular man, not given to displays of affection or spontaneity."

Caroline watched him as he stood with his back to her, his thin hands clasped behind him. He seemed to be confessing something to her. It was almost as if he felt guilty for loving Vera—as if he had betrayed his first love, art. Somehow aware that this was a very special and private moment for both of them, Caroline remained silent, fearing she might break Victor's train of thought or his mood if she spoke.

He turned then, as if sensing that she understood, and stared at her strangely. Part of him seemed to be coiled with tension, taut as a bowstring. "In the second act of the opera, when Delilah sings 'My heart at thy sweet voice,' there was a moment of such exquisite beauty that I couldn't breathe. I felt as if she were singing just for me, and I knew in that instant that I had to marry Vera. I wanted to have her as my own cherished possession and give her all the adulation that was within me. At last I had witnessed physical and artistic perfection in a living creature: Vera Solane."

Uncomfortable under Victor's unrelenting gaze, Caroline nonetheless understood for the first time why her mother had such a secure attitude about Victor. But at the same time it struck her that the man wasn't speaking of love, but rather of obsession and ownership. Didn't Victor see Vera as a human being? Didn't he see her flaws and imperfections? Surely after living with her he must be aware of her mercurial personality, maybe even suffered at the hands of it.

"I suppose you think I'm mad," Victor said, his entire attitude suddenly changing and a smile crossing his lips.

"No, of course not, Victor," she replied. "I'm happy for both of you that you found each other."

He laughed lightly. "We didn't find each other, my dear. I found *her* and I pursued her, hounded her, until

What secrets lie within the Hotel De La Marine?

For weeks the small French fishing village of Port Royal had been aflame with rumors about the mysterious stranger. Why had he come? What was he after? Challenged by his haughty, yet haunted demeanor, Marie was determined to break through his mask of indifference. But he was as charming as he was cunning, uncanny in perception and driven by vengeance. From the moment she learned his secret, Marie lived with the fear of discovery, and the thrill of danger.

Uncover those secrets with Marie in the gripping pages of *High Wind in Brittany* by *Caroline Gayet*—one of the many best-selling authors of romantic suspense presented by Mystique Books.

MYSTIQUES

Now every month you can be spellbound by 4 exciting Mystique novels like these. You'll be swept away to casinos in Monte Carlo, ski chalets in the Alps, or mysterious ruins in Mexico. You'll experience the excitement of intrigue and the warmth of romance. Mystique novels are all written by internationally acclaimed, best-selling authors of romantic suspense.

Subscribe now! As a member of the Mystiques Subscription plan, you'll receive 4 books each month. Cancel anytime. And still keep your 4 FREE BOOKS!

she consented to marry me. If it hadn't been for her illness, I often wonder if I ever would have won her."

Caroline smiled. "You make mother sound like a prize."

His expression became serious again as he answered. "But she is, Caroline. She's a trophy, the eternal flame of inimitable perfection."

"What about her moods, Victor, and her faults?" Caroline asked, trying to sound lighthearted and teasing.

Victor waved aside her question. "You may see her that way, and perhaps others do, too. But I don't question the whims of a goddess, Caroline. Sometimes," he said, a self-deprecating smile on his face. "I dream about sealing her in glass, preserving her forever. But then I would no longer have a living work of art. Have you never loved a man like that?" he asked. "No, of course not, you're still too young."

"Perhaps I'm incapable of that kind of . . . love, Victor."

"Possibly," he said quietly. "Very few people in this world would ever dedicate themselves to what they love. We live in a world of violence, I'm afraid, and people are more likely to destroy than create."

"You can't seriously believe that," Caroline replied.

"But I do. We are bombarded by vulgarity everywhere, by poor taste and crass attitudes—the weeds of destruction in a garden of loveliness. Love has been reduced to sex, and sex to lust. It has no meaning for most people any more. Beauty is envied and made plastic." He paused, and the animation in his voice disappeared. In a flat voice, he said, "Please, I could go on forever, but I can see you're tired and you must meet your friend tomorrow at the airport. You go on to bed, Caroline. I'll sit up with Vera."

"I'm not really tired," she protested.

"No, I insist."

The tone of his voice left no room for argument, and he was, after all, Vera's husband. She said good-night to Victor and left the room quietly.

As she lay on her bed, gazing at the somehow comforting Signac copy on the wall beside her, she thought of the man she had just left. She was glad to have had the opportunity to get to know Victor better, yet the intensity of the man unsettled her. Though he spoke of violence as something deplorable, Caroline couldn't quite dispel the feeling that Victor himself was capable of blind rage and uncontrollable destruction. He was obviously a passionate man, but anyone as tightly reined as he seemed to be could erupt like a volcano if provoked. Yes, he adored Vera Solane...but did he see her as little more than a breathing mural? With a last glance at Signac's tranquil harbor scene, she closed her eyes and asked herself, is that love?

SHE WAVED HAPPILY as she saw John coming through customs and ran to throw her arms around his neck even before he could put down his black overnight bag. "Johnnie! I'm so glad to see you!"

He hugged her tightly, lifting her off the floor and holding her closely. "Here, let's have a look at you," he said, putting her down. "Hmm. A little pale."

"I'm fine," she said, laughing, her shoulder-length dark brown hair shimmering in the sun-flooded terminal. "You look very dignified in that dark gray suit," she said. "Very much the Harley Street physician."

"That'll be the day," he replied, grinning. "How's your mother today?" He picked up his case with one hand, and put his arm around her waist as they began to walk to the exit.

"I don't know," she answered truthfully. "She says she's feeling a little better, but she doesn't look it. There's a sort of ashen color to her skin, and her eyes seem dull."

"Any report from the lab about her blood analysis?"

"No, not yet." Once outside she led the way toward the parking lot where she had left the Peugeot. Victor had handed her the car keys in the morning, asking only that she be back as soon as possible since he had an important errand for Alejandro. She'd remembered, then, the overheard conversation. Fleetingly, she wondered again what it had been about. But her thoughts were soon distracted by her happiness at seeing John.

Once inside the car, they made their way to the main thoroughfare in silence. Though they had often spent time alone together over the past ten years, there was something different about today. The few days she'd been gone somehow seemed much longer. She felt as if she'd learned a great deal and was much more mature.

"How does it feel to drive on the right-hand side of the road?" John asked, almost absently.

She smiled. "Strange. And I still haven't got my signals straight. I feel as if I should turn left when I signal right."

"Drive slowly, then," he teased. "Other than this illness, how's it going between you and your mother?"

"All right," Caroline replied. "Oh, there are some

awkward moments, but that's to be expected. I've met her new husband, Victor."

"Oh? What's he like?" He rested his hand softly on her forearm, asking, "Can you drive and talk at the same time?"

"Of course!" Caroline laughed then became serious again. "About Victor . . . he's a funny one, I think. Completely the opposite of mother."

"How so?"

She tilted her head to one side. "I'm not really sure," she answered. "Mother's theatrical, of course, and he's not. Oh, John," she rushed on, "I've learned so much about her in the past few days. She's had a much more difficult life than I would ever have guessed. She's really had to work hard to rise to the top."

"And Victor?"

Caroline risked a quick sidelong glance at her companion. "Fire and ice," she said tersely.

"I beg your pardon?"

"He's . . . well, I suppose you could say he's like a dormant volcano. On the outside, he's quiet and serene, but on the inside. . . ." She hesitated before going on. "Oh, I don't know."

John nodded to himself. "Well, I suppose it would take a very unusual man to want to marry your mother."

"John!"

"I didn't mean it that way. What I meant was that any man who'd marry a famous woman has to be unusual. But, of course, she has retired, and that would make a difference."

"Wouldn't you marry a well-known woman," she asked, half joking and half in earnest.

"I suppose it would depend on the woman," he replied. "Do they seem happy?"

"I can't tell yet," she answered honestly. "They're both so unusual that it's difficult to judge."

"I was afraid you'd say that. You're not at all comfortable with them, are you?" he asked. "Look, Caroline, why don't you come back with me tomorrow. I'm sure your mother will be fine. Frankly part of my reason for agreeing to see her was to convince you of the folly of this visit."

"What do you mean?"

"Caroline, I want you to know that I do understand why you wanted to come back to Spain. But I think you should face it: you don't belong among these people. Vera Solane is your biological mother, but that's all. She comes from another world, another way of life. England is your home, with me—with all of us," he added quickly.

"Johnnie," she said slowly, "you must stop worrying about me all the time. I can look after myself, really."

"But you'll get hurt, Caroline. You're so terribly vulnerable. You're not ready to be among the idle rich and partying jet-setters."

She had to laugh. "Mother is hardly the idle rich, John, and Victor has earned his wealth—he didn't inherit it."

"Even so. We're your real family, not by blood, but because we care about you."

"I know, Johnnie, but surely you can understand why this holiday with mother is so important to me," Caroline replied.

He sighed heavily. "Yes, I suppose so. But still . . . ."

"Look, those are the spires of the Church of the *Sagrada Familia*," she said suddenly, pointing to her left.

"You're changing the subject," he said perceptively.

Caroline smiled. "Yes, because there's nothing more to discuss. I'm doing what I have to do, John." She took her right hand from the wheel and placed it gently over his. "It's sweet of you to be so worried, but it'll be all right, you'll see."

"I hope so, Caroline. For both our sakes."

She was tempted to ask him what he meant, but thought better of it. If she didn't ask him, he wouldn't be able to lecture to her with his big brother sternness.

"Isn't Barcelona beautiful?" she said. "If you'll stay awhile longer, I can show you some of the sights instead of just this glimpse from the highway."

"I can't stay longer, Caroline, and I don't think Spain is as beautiful as you are."

"John! You've never paid me a compliment before!"

"You were never away before," he replied simply.

Chapter 9

Alejandro was pacing in the front garden as the Peugeot pulled up, so Caroline didn't even bother to turn off the engine. Silently, his face devoid of expression, the servant got into the car the moment she and John were out of it.

"Who's he?"

"A chauffeur," Caroline explained. "Mother says he's been with Victor for years and years. He's a deaf-mute, which is why I didn't introduce you."

"Not a very pleasant fellow, is he," John commented as they climbed the stairs to the veranda. "But then, that nasty scar on his face doesn't help."

"Don't worry, he's hardly ever around. This is only the second time I've seen him, as a matter of fact. But look at the house, Johnnie...and the view! Isn't it spectacular?"

He smiled at her. "Yes, Caroline, it is. Really, I mean it."

"Wait till you see the inside," she continued enthusiastically as they entered the front hall.

"Don't you think it might be a good idea if I took a look at your mother first?"

"Oh, yes, of course," Caroline said contritely. It wasn't like her to be so selfish, but she had to admit that she was delighted to see John and probably just wanted to show off a bit. She started up the broad stairway, but stopped as she saw Patrick who was standing at the top of the landing. There was almost a scowl on his rugged face as he looked down at Caroline and John.

"Pat, this is Dr. John Clarke," she said slowly, wondering if Pat had had an argument with her mother. He was wearing his work clothes and his muslin shirt was open halfway down his chest, revealing his darkly tanned, taut skin.

"How do you do," Pat said coolly. As he stepped down toward them, he seemed to remember his manners and put out his right hand. "I'm Pat O'Flaherty."

John nodded, a faint smile on his lips as if he, too, sensed that something was amiss. "Nice to meet you."

"John's flown in from England to examine mother."

"So Victor told me. He's with her now, waiting for you. Where's your luggage?" Pat asked John.

"I only brought an overnight bag," John answered. "I won't be here longer than that. It's by the front door."

Patrick nodded. "Only the guest room has been decorated," he said. "It's that one," he added, indicating the door behind him with a jerk of his thumb.

"I'll show it to him later, Pat," Caroline said, baffled by his cold, almost rude attitude. He stood aside as she led the way upstairs to her mother's room. A few moments later, she heard the front door close loudly. *I wonder what's bothering him*, she thought. Could it be that he regetted his openness of the previous night? Or was he just tired after a late night and a full morning of work?

As she opened the door to her mother's suite, she forced herself to put Pat's strange behavior out of her mind. Victor was seated next to Vera's bed, and Caroline quickly made the introductions. Then she excused herself so John could proceed with his examination, followed by Victor seconds later. They waited together in the sitting room.

"Why's Pat acting so strangely?" She tried to make her question sound casual.

"Is he? I hadn't noticed," Victor replied. "I told him this morning that your mother was ill, and he came up to pay his respects. But he seemed all right to me."

He was so obviously preoccupied with Vera's condition that Caroline let the subject drop. Muffled sounds came from the bedroom as John asked questions and Vera responded. She wondered what John thought of her mother, now that he'd finally met her. He certainly wasn't seeing her at her best, but Caroline guessed that Vera was going out of her way to charm him. If so, John wouldn't stand a chance.

"I think I'll go for a walk, Victor, if you don't mind."

"Go ahead," he said. "Lunch will be at one, as usual, but you have time."

Feeling useless and still a little perturbed by Pat's behavior, Caroline left the room and went downstairs. Consuelo was in the dining room setting the table as

Caroline passed on her way to the front door. Quietly, she let herself out.

She began to stroll aimlessly through the front gardens, hoping that John had been right; that her mother's condition was nothing more than a touch of food poisoning. But what if it was something serious, she asked herself. *Wouldn't it be ironic*, she thought, *if, after all this time, just when I'm finally getting to know her, she were terminally ill?* No sooner had the thought entered her mind than Caroline paused, shocked at herself. It was so unfeeling and heartless to think of her mother's death as merely "ironic."

Then it struck her; she really didn't love her mother. She loved the concept, the idea of having a mother, but she didn't even know Vera Solane. It felt strange to admit it, yet at the same time somehow liberating. All those years of clinging to the hope that she and her mother would one day be reunited, find a relationship they'd never had before...and now Caroline knew that it had been nothing more than childish fantasy. Of course she cared about her mother. Vera was a human being and the woman who'd given birth to her. But how would she feel if Vera were to die? Bereft? Heartbroken? No, she had to concede. *I'd feel disappointed*, she realized, *even sorry for both of us. But how could I miss someone I never knew?*

Once again, she'd reached the rose gardens her father had tended so lovingly. The tall hedges still protected them from the breezes from the sea, and in the daylight, she could see the stone bench that she'd sat on the night she'd felt the strange vibration. Caroline let her mind wander as she gazed out across the promontory to the sparkling Mediterranean, dotted with distant sail-boats.

Then she again felt the earth beneath her begin to tremble slightly. Perplexed, she tried to think of what might be causing it. Though she was quite near the house, it wasn't air conditioned, so she knew that wasn't the reason for the vibrations.

Curiosity made her rise and walk toward the end of the path. At the end of the path she'd have good view of what was going on below at the base of the cliff. Perhaps the area was being excavated? But when she reached the edge, she saw nothing that would explain the noise, no heavy equipment or trucks. She walked back toward the bench, still baffled, then realized that the trembling had stopped. What on earth could it be? Where was it coming from? Remembering Pat's sarcasm the last time, she vowed she wouldn't ask him. But if she didn't ask Pat, who could she ask?

Caroline glanced at her watch and realized that John would be just about finished with his examination. The mystery would have to wait, she thought as she made her way back to the house. Maybe she'd ask Victor about the strange vibrations—perhaps he'd know.

WHEN SHE ENTERED the living room, John was speaking to Victor, and Caroline couldn't help being rather amused in spite of the gravity of the situation. She'd never seen John in his role as a doctor, and it was difficult to reconcile the Johnnie she knew with this solemn, authoritative young man talking with Victor.

"I'm reasonably convinced it's food poisoning," he was saying. "However I'll need to know the results of the blood analysis before I can be absolutely certain. Can you contact the local physician and ask him to prod the lab?"

Victor shook his head. "I'm afraid, Dr. Clarke, that my Spanish is limited to hello and goodbye."

"I'll call him," Caroline volunteered as she joined John on the eight-foot-long velvet couch. "But you're sure it's nothing serious, aren't you?"

He looked at her, his gray eyes reassuring. "Yes."

"What I can't understand," Victor said, "is why Vera became ill and I didn't. We both had the same thing for supper."

"It happens quite frequently," John said. "A steak or a fillet of sole—whatever—doesn't go bad all at once. Portions begin to be tainted in different places. The part you ate might have been fine, whereas what Mrs. O'Flaherty had wasn't."

Victor's blue eyes took on an expression Caroline couldn't quite fathom. If she hadn't known how devoted he was to Vera, Caroline might have interpreted the expression as one of smug satisfaction, as if Victor were actually pleased about John's explanation.

"Well," he said, taking an antique pocket watch from his vest and snapping open the lid, "it's about twenty minutes before lunch will be served. Why don't you show the doctor his room, Caroline, and then you can call the local physician while Dr. Clarke is washing up." He closed his watch and looked at Caroline. "I'll be in my den should you need me for anything."

She watched him leave the leaving room and wondered if Victor had been sent to military school as a youth. His bearing and posture were as ramrod stiff as a British honor guard's.

"I see what you mean," John said, standing up. "He's very tense, isn't he?"

As they climbed the stairs, Caroline asked, "Well, what do you think of Vera Solane?"

"Formidable," John replied, laughing. "But she is, as you said, fascinating. A willful child one moment, and a seductive charmer the next. But I agree with you, Caroline. I don't think there's a malicious bone in her body. She's obviously a selfish person, but doesn't mean to harm anyone."

Caroline smiled, pleased that John had been able to perceive so much in such a brief time. "It's just that mother doesn't think ahead," she said. "At least that's the way it seems to me."

John put his overnight bag down on top of the oak bureau in the guest room, then he turned to her, placing his hands on her shoulders. "Very few people ever think ahead, Caroline. If they did, there wouldn't be so much stupidity and cruelty in the world. I'm afraid most people are just impulsive, and your mother is no exception."

"It's one of the things I've always admired about you, Johnnie," Caroline said. "You're very methodical about life, always weighing the possible outcome of a decision before you act on it."

He smiled slowly. "Some people might find that too predictable and boring."

She shook her head. "No, it's reassuring. It means you're levelheaded and dependable."

"Whereas you have a charming combination of both qualities." John smiled. "You can think matters through with the detachment of a field marshal, yet other times you're completely spontaneous—like when you made the decision to accept your mother's invitation to come here."

Caroline moved away from him then, a small frown on her oval face. "That was something I simply had to do, John. Can't I ever convince you of how important it was, and is, to me? In my mind I had an incomplete portrait of the woman who is my mother. I had sketched in the basic outlines, but there were no details, no colors, no nuance of expression. I had to discover who she really was and fill in the features that make her different from anyone else."

John sighed. "Yes, I know. I suppose I just can't stop worrying about you."

She came back to the center of the room and put her hand on his cheek. "You're a dear, Johnnie, but you're being overly protective." Then she sensed again that there was something he wanted to say. She knew better than to try to prompt him—John always withdrew when coaxed—so she resigned herself to waiting until he found the words to express himself.

"Well, I suppose I'd best freshen up before lunch," she said finally. "Victor means it when he says twenty minutes. He keeps Foxdale on a rigid time schedule. I don't think even the German railroads are as precise!"

LUNCH WAS A STRAINED occasion, even though Caroline made every effort to keep conversation flowing smoothly. Victor was taciturn, which was only natural, given his concern for Vera. But it was Patrick who'd really cast the pall over the meal. He was only a hair's breadth away from sullen.

She tried to draw him out several times but finally

gave up. They'd had a lovely time the evening before, and Pat had been warm and outgoing. Then, when he'd kissed her goodnight, he'd been tender and gentle. What had happened between last night and this morning, Caroline couldn't even begin to guess. Each time she looked across the table at Pat's tanned, rugged face—which only made John's English pallor more pronounced—she became increasingly baffled. His black lashes seemed to veil his hazel eyes, and his thick eyebrows were drawn together in anger. It was as if he were refusing to look at her for fear he'd do something terrible.

Finally, grateful that coffee was being served and the ordeal would be over soon, Caroline turned to Victor. "I've been meaning to ask you about something unusual in the rose garden," she said.

"Unusual?"

"Yes, there's a kind of rumbling vibration underground, which seems to come and go."

Victor stiffened almost imperceptibly and his blue eyes took on that distant cold look Caroline was learning to expect. "You must be mistaken, Caroline, dear."

"No, I'm very sure about it, Victor."

Patrick snorted. "She tried that one out on me, too," he said. "I found her on her hands and knees in the dark on Saturday night."

"Really?" Victor stirred his coffee with apparently idle interest. "It must have been a passing truck," he added, turning back to Caroline.

She paused for a moment to consider Victor's comment, then said, "No, I doubt it. I'm sure I would have heard the truck's engine grinding to get up our hill.

Besides, why would a truck come up this way, any-how?"

"I really wouldn't know," Victor answered, an amused smile on his thin lips. "But it makes far more sense than a patch of ground rumbling continually."

Caroline looked at Victor closely and had the strong impression that he knew more than he was revealing. While she couldn't be certain, it seemed to her that Victor was trying to conceal something. There was no way she could prove it, of course, but Caroline had come to be suspicious whenever Victor's eyes took on that icy unreadable glaze.

Aware of the lengthening silence, Caroline said, "I made no mention of the vibrations being continual, Victor. I've only noticed it twice, but it's happened each time I've been in the rose garden. Since Pat refuses to take me seriously," she went on, "I thought I'd ask you."

Pat tossed his napkin onto the table. "I guess theatrics run in the family, Victor," he said sarcastically.

"Let's not overlook the fact that my father was an engineer!" Her words had come out more hotly than she'd intended, but Pat's attitude was annoying her.

"Why don't you show me around, Caroline," John put in, plainly trying to prevent an argument.

"That's an excellent idea," Victor concurred. "Disagreement is bad for the digestion," he added with a cool smile.

Angry and a little embarrassed that no one believed her, Caroline led the way out through the French doors in the dining room. The water in a circular fountain, made with colorful mosaic tiles, gurgled soothingly.

"I'd like to check out your rose garden," John said

when they were far enough away from the house not to be overheard.

"So you can make fun of me, too?"

"Don't be defensive," he admonished gently. "Maybe I can figure out what's going on."

Chapter 10

Caroline smiled ruefully at John and they both straightened from their crouched positions. The rose garden was stubbornly free from any vibrations or rumblings. They retired to the bench and absently began talking about the history of the area—of the ancient Greeks who'd settled there, the conquest by the armies of Caesar in 44 B.C., how the Arabs and the Moors had influenced the culture. They gradually covered everything Caroline could remember her father having taught her as a girl.

Though John was politely attentive, Caroline knew they were both only killing time, waiting for the ground to tremble. It didn't.

John took out his pipe, tamping tobacco into it. "It's pretty clear," he said, striking a match, "that you love Catalonia. I'd no idea you were so well versed in its history."

"What you really want to say," she responded, more than a little disappointed and feeling foolish, "is that we've been here for about a half hour and nothing's happened to substantiate my remarks at lunch."

"No, that's not true, Caroline. You're feeling defensive, which I can understand. Let's go for a walk. We can come back this way afterward. All right?"

She smiled slowly. "You're the most patient man I've ever known."

"Really?" He took her by the elbow and they began to walk back past the hedges, toward the still-unrestored vineyards behind the villa. "You sound very knowledgeable," he said, laughing lightly. "How many men have you known that well?"

She threw back her head as if she were silently counting them, just to tease him. Then, seeing the concerned expression on his face, she stopped pretending. "The only two men I've known well are my father and you. You're perfectly aware that I've rarely dated anyone more than two or three times, so I can hardly say I know them well."

"You had me worried there for a second," John said. "I was beginning to imagine some sort of sordid secret life none of us suspected."

Caroline laughed. "Can you imagine anyone getting past your mother with that kind of nonsense?"

"No. You have a good point there," he agreed.

They strolled on in silence for a few minutes, and she remembered that she always felt comfortable in John's company. Then, impetuously, she asked, "Would you like to go down to the cove? I know of a path that's been cut out of the side of the cliff. . . ."

"In my good Sunday suit?" he asked, pretending to be horrified.

"Don't be so stuffy," she teased. "You can roll up your

trouser legs when we get down there. Come on! It's beautiful and you may never come back here again."

"I don't know, Caroline. This is really the only good suit I've got, and—"

"I'll race you!" she called, beginning to run closer to the edge of the cliff.

"Hey! Wait for me!"

Caroline saw an almond grove ahead of her on the lower slope and remembered that beyond it was a rock ledge that marked the start of the steep path down to the sea. She knew she'd have to let John catch up with her or he'd get lost in the grove, so she slowed down. Grateful for the chance to catch her breath, she watched as John came running toward her, his jacket in his left hand, a corner of his sedately striped tie exposed in the pocket. He was out of breath when he reached her.

"I can't remember when I last ran anywhere," he said, panting.

"Then you should do it more often, doctor," she answered. "Quite obviously, sir, you're not in fit condition!" She tried very hard to imitate John's professional tone.

He grinned weakly. "I daresay you're right. Now, where to from here?"

Pointing, Caroline said, "Through those trees."

John's brows rose questioningly. "It's a bit of a walk, isn't it?"

"Don't be such an old man, Johnnie," she teased. "It's not all that far, and it really is worth it."

She led the way through the grove, welcoming the shade from the hot June sun. When they reached the rock ledge and looked down to the beach below, Caroline realized that she'd forgotten just how steep the path was. Yet, rather than have John think she was a coward, she gamely began to descend the narrow route, albeit slowly and carefully.

"Caroline! You don't seriously mean to climb down there!"

She stopped and glanced back up at him, smiling at his appalled expression. In a way, Caroline couldn't blame him; the route down was nothing more than crudely leveled rocks with a sheer drop below it. "Are you scared, Dr. Clarke?"

"Frankly, yes," he said.

Caroline gazed down at the gleaming white beach and the frothing green sea lapping gently against the enormous boulders that dotted the sand. "It's not the fall that'll hurt you," she called to him, laughing. "It's the sudden stop!"

John shook his head with amused tolerance. "That's a very old joke," he said. "Well, if you can do it, so can I."

"Sidestep your way down, Johnnie and hold onto the rocks so you don't lose your footing."

Cautiously, Caroline continued on down, enjoying the feel of the rough stones on her palms and feeling exhilarated as the breezes whipped through her dark brown hair. Gulls circled nearby, squealing as they glided and swooped closer to the water. She glanced back to see how John was faring and noticed that he'd tied the sleeves of his suit jacket around his waist to leave his hands free. He appeared to be very nervous but determined, and she had to admit he was being a very good sport.

When they reached the bottom, John heaved a sigh of

relief. "I suppose this was your secret hideaway as a child," he said, pushing a lock of curly hair out of his eyes.

Caroline nodded. "It's practically inaccessible, so I had it all to myself. The only way to get here is to swim in or bring a rowboat ashore."

John undid the sleeves of his coat and folded it neatly on a nearby rock. Then he bent over and removed his shoes and socks, rolling up his pant cuffs neatly. When he straightened, he no longer looked like a stern physician. He was just a young carefree man having a good time. "If I'd known it was going to be like this," he said, rolling up his shirtsleeves, "I'd have brought a bottle of wine and some cheese, then I'd read you my poetry."

"You don't write poetry!"

He shrugged. "Not anymore, but I used to. At one point it seemed monumentally important to understand the meaning of life, and my relation to the cosmos," he said, grinning. "Endless droning poems flowed from my pen as I tried to harness the universe within my adolescent brain."

"You never told me," she chided as they began to walk along the water's edge, the sea gently washing their bare feet.

"Not even mother knows," he said. "Do you think I wanted everyone laughing at me?"

"But maybe they were good, maybe you have a real talent."

John laughed. "Not to worry. I reread some of them about a year ago. They were terrible—I threw them away."

"What? Oh, Johnnie! How could you! Wasn't it like destroying a part of yourself!"

He stopped walking and suddenly became very serious. "No, not really. But I've since discovered something else that makes me feel that way."

Caroline knew him well enough to realize that he was now ready to express what he'd been unable to say earlier. She looked up at him and saw a look on his face she'd never seen before.

"I've. . . well, I now know that life without you is very empty and meaningless, Caroline. No, don't interrupt, let me finish."

She watched him as he led her by the hand to a shady spot nestled near the base of the cliff. They sat down, and she waited quietly for John to gather his thoughts. Caroline felt a murmur of excitement at what she knew he was about to say and wondered briefly why she had never viewed John as a possible suitor.

He held her hand, stroking it lightly. "I've always liked you very much, Caroline. You were very brave when you first came to live with us. You accepted being dumped with strangers with a proud determination, and I admired your pluck enormously."

"I remember how you used to try to cheer me up whenever I got depressed or upset," Caroline said, almost whispering.

John smiled shyly. "The discrepancy in our ages isn't noticeable now, but then, when you were only ten and I was fourteen. . .well, it made a big difference. I've watched you grow up with Lucy and Anne and realized that you really had no friends your own age. They were both far too young for you. . .and I was too old."

"If I'd stayed with my mother, I wouldn't have had anyone," she remarked sincerely.

"Perhaps. But until you went away last Friday, I admit that I took your presence pretty much for granted. Maybe if mother and the girls hadn't gone away, I wouldn't have missed you quite so much. But, left alone in the house, I had to face facts. I'm in love with you, Caroline. Perhaps I have been for a long time and didn't even realize it . . . but I know it now. I want you to come home to Hampstead and marry me."

"I . . . I don't know what to say."

He shook his head. "Don't say anything right now. I understand that you want to spend more time here with your mother, but I had to let you know how I felt. We could have a very good life, Caroline, with a great deal to share and enjoy. We already have a lot in common," he concluded persuasively.

For some obscure reason, John's last remark brought Patrick O'Flaherty to Caroline's mind. Filled with self-reproach for listening to one man's proposal and thinking of another, Caroline leaned closer to John and stroked his unruly hair. "Kiss me, John," she said softly.

He leaned toward her, putting his arm around her waist and gently bringing her to him. John's lips pressed against hers lightly, as if he didn't want to shock her or go too quickly. Caroline could feel his torso resting gently against her body and tried to conjur up an appropriate response to his nearness, his kiss. She wanted to *feel* something in John's arms; a tingling, butterflies—all the things she'd read about in books that indicated love and desire.

Instead, her mind recalled the mocking laughter of Patrick O'Flaherty as she had stalked away from his kiss the day after she'd arrived. She remembered how she'd given herself up to his lips involuntarily, before she'd

caught herself. And she thought of the pleasurable evening they'd had together in Badelona, and the way he'd
kissed her that night, tenderly, sweetly, his strong broad
hands caressing her. . . .

Caroline felt nothing in John's arms.

WHEN THEY RETURNED to the house, John was beaming
proudly, as if she'd already consented to marry him.
Feeling guilty, Caroline was glad that Patrick was
nowhere in sight. Despite his rudeness earlier, she didn't
want to be in the same room with Pat and John simultaneously—not for a while, anyway. She feared that
she'd make comparisons between the two men and didn't
want to risk seeing John in a less favorable light.

As she and John crossed the foyer, Victor called to
her. "Caroline, would you come here for a few moments, please?"

"Certainly," she answered, crossing over to where
Victor stood in the doorway to the living room. "I'll see
you later, John," she said over her shoulder.

Victor closed the double doors once she was inside. "I'd
like to have a little chat with you," he began solemnly.

"Is something wrong?"

"Possibly," he replied, sitting across from her in the
wingback chair. "Vera is in a very poor frame of mind,
and I'm worried about her. I haven't seen her in that
state since she first lost her voice. I don't know how
much she's told you, Caroline, but when the doctors ad-
vised her that she'd have to rest her singing voice for
more than a year, your mother fell apart."

"A nervous breakdown?"

Victor folded his hands and stared down at them. "She

wasn't sick enough to be institutionalized, but she had to spend more than a month in a rest home. She would be manic one moment, screaming invectives and hurling things across the room, and the next she'd retreat within herself, weeping silently. It nearly broke my heart to see her like that," he explained, then lifted his blue eyes. "It had nothing to do with insanity, you understand. Her entire world had just been taken away from her, and the shock was more than she could bear."

Caroline returned his steady gaze, perplexed. "And you think this is happening again?"

"I don't know," he replied with a sigh. "While you were out with your friend, I went upstairs to see how she was feeling. She began to rant about how stupid all doctors are, accusing me of enjoying her illness. . . ."

"Oh no!"

He nodded sadly. "She did the same thing the last time. But then she began to cry about your being here at Foxdale, how guilty she feels for not having raised you herself, the years that've been lost. She wants you to stay here, Caroline."

"But I'm going to," she said quickly, wondering how she could help her mother. "I'll be here all summer."

"No, my dear, that's not what she means. She wants you to move back here and live with us permanently. She's tormenting herself needlessly, we both know that . . . but she wants to atone for the past."

The possibility of staying permanently had not entered Caroline's head, and she didn't quite know how to answer her stepfather. She only had one more year at school before graduation, then she would have to find a job and begin her career. How could she possibly abandon all her hard work and move back to Badalona?

Caroline stood up and crossed over to the windows overlooking the sparkling sea, her mind racing with contradictory thoughts.

"Vera needs you, Caroline," Victor said quietly. "It won't be forever, I promise; just until she's completely back to normal again. Frankly, I now think the cause of her present illness is emotional, not physical."

She turned around to speak to Victor again and noted that the Cézanne was no longer on the far wall. Instead, there was a watercolor by an artist she didn't recognize. Then, she saw that the Rouault and the Rousseau were also gone, replaced by works she wasn't familiar with. She put aside the distraction and willed herself to concentrate on Victor's proposition. "I'll have to think about it, Victor. It's very kind of you to ask me to stay on indefinitely, and I'm touched by your concern for mother. However, it's a very big decision."

"Yes, I appreciate that," he said. "And I know you have your studies to think about as well. But don't forget that the University of Barcelona has an excellent art department, and there are quite a few superb painters in the area who tutor. It would mean transferring and studying in Spanish, but I don't think that would prove too difficult for you."

She moved back to the center of the room, noticing the tired lines around Victor's eyes. "I'll need some time to think it over," she repeated. "A few days, maybe a week."

He rose and put his arm around her shoulder. "Of course."

On her way to the door, she paused to look around the room. "What happened to the paintings?" she asked, mildly curious.

"Oh, I put these up for a change," her stepfather

replied. "I like to rotate the paintings for variety. If you look at the same work in the same place all the time, you begin to take it for granted, and soon you don't even see it anymore."

"I hadn't thought of that," she said. "I guess you're right." Smiling faintly, she left the room.

Caroline paused for a moment in the foyer and leaned against the door. She wondered just how serious her mother's condition might be. She had known that her mother was temperamental, but she hadn't even considered the possibility that Vera had suffered a nervous breakdown, much less that she might be on the verge of a relapse. What Victor wanted her to do was no small favor, and Caroline knew she would have to weigh the matter carefully. Fortunately John was nearby, and she would be able to discuss the plan with him. Then she remembered that John had proposed that afternoon. She strongly doubted that he could be objective at this point and decided it would be best not to say anything for the moment.

As she walked into the hallway leading to her room, she saw Alejandro disappearing through the door at the far end. He glanced furtively through the tinted glass in the door, and their eyes locked for a scant moment before he turned away. Something in his look made her suspicious.

Caroline frowned. What was Alejandro doing in this part of the house? Had he been in her room?

Chapter 11

Caroline entered her room half expecting to see it ransacked. She knew it was unfair to judge Alejandro on the basis of his dour scarred appearance, but she couldn't help it.

At first glance everything seemed in place. Caroline walked across to her bureau and opened the top drawer, where she kept her leather jewelry case. She didn't have anything terribly valuable, but over the last few years she'd managed to collect some attractive nine-karat rose gold from the Victorian period at the antique stalls on London's Portobello Road. Though she was terribly fond of the few bracelets and necklaces, Caroline strongly doubted that they'd be worth very much to a thief. Besides, why would Alejandro have to stoop to that sort of thing? Having been in Victor's employ for so many years, surely he received a good wage and felt secure in his job....

A quick survey of the leather box showed nothing was

missing, and Caroline stood staring into the drawer for a few moments. Then her eye fell on her passport case, where she kept all her important documents for the trip. If contained a letter of credit with the local bank, her student card and other assorted pieces of identification. Suddenly she remembered reading that British passports had a high black-market value, and she opened the case. But it was still there.

The discovery should have reassured her, but for some reason her suspicions deepened. She quickly went through her other drawers, looking to see if anything was out of place or missing. Then she moved to the dressing table and inspected the articles there, but everything seemed to be in perfect order. She sat down on the edge of her bed in an attempt to calm herself.

Maybe she was just imagining things. After all, she had been through a lot of emotional turmoil in the last few days at Foxdale. Her mother's revelations, and now her illness, were weighing heavily on Caroline's mind. And then there was Victor and his surprising plan to have her live with them. Could she really contemplate living with a woman she hardly knew and a man whose pent-up emotions seemed on the verge of erupting?

Gradually her confusion turned into anger. Why was she, neglected by her mother as a child, now expected to change her whole life, just to make Vera happy? Surely that was asking too much. Wasn't her mother merely acting true to form—arranging her little make-believe world to her own satisfaction?

Caroline slumped back onto the bed as tears formed in the corners of her eyes. It was all so complicated. Then she remembered Johnnie and what he had said on the beach earlier. She smiled as she thought of him.

He was a good, steady friend, someone she could trust and go to when she needed help. Then she realized that he was just a friend—not a lover. Her thoughts immediately went to Pat. She couldn't pin it down yet, but she knew there was a world of difference in her feelings toward him. Despite Pat's proprietary attitude about Foxdale and despite the sarcasm which often colored her time with him, the evening at the *cantina* in Badalona had convinced her that she wanted to get to know him better.

But what did Pat think of her? If today's behavior was any indication, the answer was "not much." Maybe she should follow in her mother's footsteps and marry Johnnie for the security he was offering her. The thought gave her a new insight into her mother's motivations.

Still confused, but feeling somewhat calmer, Caroline rose from the bed, deciding to visit her mother. As she turned to straighten the covers, she noticed that the Signac painting was missing. In its place was a new painting of questionable quality by an unknown artist.

So Alejandro *had* been in her room, but he had not been searching for valuables. But why had he switched the painting? Then she recalled Victor's words: "If you look at the same work in the same place all the time, you begin to take it for granted." That might make sense for Victor, who perhaps had become too accustomed to the lovely copies around him, but it irritated Caroline, who had come to enjoy waking up to the sight of the fog-shrouded harbor scene. Why would Victor order Alejandro to switch the painting in her room, when it was only

Caroline who would notice? She would ask him later, she decided.

She ran a comb through her hair and repaired her tear-stained eye makeup before leaving her room. As she walked up the stairs and into the hallway leading to her mother's room, she noticed that most of the paintings on the walls there had been changed as well. There wasn't a single picture she recognized, which struck her as very odd since Victor seemed so fond of his copies of the Impressionist masters. Why the sudden change to contemporary works, all by unknowns? She presumed he had stored the others in the attic, but was not in any mood to give this eccentricity any serious thought.

At the door to the master suite, she knocked lightly. Not sure if her mother could hear her or not, she went in and called out, "Mother? Are you awake?"

"Yes, dear. Come in, come in," she replied from the bedroom.

Caroline went into the room and had to adjust her eyes to the dim light. "Why don't you let the sunlight in, mother? It's so gloomy in here!" She started to cross over to the windows, but Vera stopped her.

"No, please don't," she said almost in a whimper.

"But...."

"No, Caroline, I insist. Indulge me, please. I've no makeup on and I feel gray and dingy. I don't want anyone to see me like this."

Smiling at her mother's vanity, Caroline nonetheless didn't argue further. "Are you feeling any better?"

"A little," Vera said. "Your doctor friend gave me some medicine, and it's eased the cramps. He seems a very nice young man, though I admit I don't have the confidence in his medical expertise you seem to have."

Caroline sat down across from her mother. "Right now," she said, laughing lightly, "you wouldn't have confidence in any physician. John is an excellent doctor. Perhaps even more importantly, he's not afraid to admit when he's baffled and is quick to call in another opinion. You couldn't be in better hands, mother."

Vera nodded slowly. "I suppose you're right, dear. It's just that...well, I had never been sick a day in my life until I lost my voice. I suppose it's made me wary. I feel as if some new catastrophe might occur."

"That's nothing but superstitious thinking," Caroline said softly. "What could possibly happen?"

"I don't know," Vera answered wistfully. "Flood, famine, pestilence...."

"Oh mother," Caroline responded, laughing. Then, changing the subject, she asked, "Is there something I can get for you? A book or magazine to while away the time?"

"Then I'd have to turn on a light. No, thank you. How's Victor taking my illness?" she inquired.

"He's worried about you, needless to say. Maybe that's why he's changing all the pictures around to give himself something to do. I suppose he's storing them all in the attic."

"I doubt that," Vera said. "It's still sealed off. When your father died, I put everything in the house up there and had it boarded up. Victor's probably got them all in his den, deciding what to do with them." She toyed absently with the edge of the blanket. "Are you getting along with him all right?" she asked hesitantly.

"Certainly," Caroline answered. "He told me this afternoon that you've been feeling depressed and would like me to stay on at Foxdale permanently."

Vera's large brown eyes looked surprised. "I never said that," she commented. "You have your education to finish and your own life to lead. Perhaps Victor misunderstood me. While I'd love it if you stayed and considered this your home, I wouldn't ask you to uproot yourself after all these years. I admit I'm selfish, Caroline, but I'm not insane," she said, a perplexed expression on her face.

Caroline leaned back in her chair, wondering how Victor could have been so wrong about her mother's wishes. But then, perhaps Victor was just trying to guess what would make Vera happy, whether she'd said anything or not.

"I'm so annoyed about getting sick," Vera said after a moment. "It's just wasting the precious time you and I could be spending together."

"You didn't exactly plan it," Caroline said goodnaturedly. "Besides, you'll be up and well in no time. Then we can continue to put Foxdale back in shape."

"How long will Dr. Clarke be here?" her mother asked, changing the subject.

"He's leaving tomorrow. He's waiting to get the lab results just to be sure you're going to be all right, and then he'll return to England."

"John's very fond of you I noticed. Any time your name was mentioned this morning his entire attitude seemed to perk up."

Caroline nodded, then decided to share her secret. "He proposed to me today," she said softly.

"Darling! How wonderful!" Vera sat up in bed, her eyes sparkling happily. "And did you accept?"

"No, not yet. I want to think about it. I'm not at all sure I'm ready to get married right now. I'd like a chance to develop a career of my own. Not only that, I also feel that I haven't dated enough men to trust my judgment in such a serious matter."

"Oh, you're so right, my dear," Vera said. "I know it's fashionable to get divorces these days, but I still think it would be better if people thought things over first, before jumping into a marriage destined to fail. Some people seem to think that after the wedding vows, life will all be roses and caviar. Then they get bored with each other and wonder why."

She reached out for Caroline's hand before continuing. "As you know, I didn't get married until I was twenty-seven, with my career firmly on its way. I might never have married if your father hadn't been such a dear, persistent man. He made it clear that he understood my plans perfectly, that he'd never resent having to share me with an audience. I believe it's terribly important to know just who you are, what you want from life and where you want to be before you take on the responsibilities of marriage. And that takes a few years of being in the real world, being self-sufficient—believe me."

Caroline smiled. "I don't think John would stop me from having a job, though we haven't talked about it. But since he's a doctor, his schedule would have to take precedence over mine, and I don't know if I'm ready for that."

"Dear girl, if you're asking yourself all these questions, then John's not the man for you. When you've met the right one, there'll be nothing to stop you from wanting to marry him. Love is eternal optimism, Caroline, and when two people work toward the same goals, most difficulties can be sorted through."

"Well, as I said, I haven't given John an answer yet."

"Smart girl."

"It's funny," Caroline said casually. "Sometimes, when you and I are alone, I feel very comfortable with you, as if I'd known you all these years. And then, like now, it comes back to me that we don't know each other at all."

"Yes, I've felt that, too," Vera said quietly.

"Am I what you expected me to be?"

"In what way?" Vera asked, propping herself up in bed as if readying herself for a long conversation.

"Oh, my appearance, my opinions, that sort of thing."

Vera's lips pursed as she thought about it. "Yes, I think so...except you're infinitely more blunt and direct than I ever dreamed of being."

"The English upbringing, perhaps," Caroline suggested, amused.

"No doubt. Of course, physically, you're exactly what I thought you'd look like. You're practically a perfect mixture of your father and me, and miraculously you got the best features from both of us. I'd have recognized you in the middle of Times Square on New Year's Eve!"

"You're joking!"

"No, I'm not." Vera replied seriously. "But as for your intellect, your attitudes, I don't know what I thought you'd be like. More like your father, I suppose, since you spent so much time with him. I'll have to get to know you much better before I have any firm opinions about that." She touched her hair lightly and smiled. "You know, dear, I *am* feeling much better now. I may even get up and join you for dinner this evening."

"I'll ask John if that would be all right," Caroline said.

"And what about you, Caroline. Am I what you expected?" her mother asked, a tremor in her voice.

"Well, since I saw your picture in the paper or in magazines, I knew what you looked like. I'd already decided years ago that you had a terrible temper, cared about nothing but yourself—that sort of thing. The stereotype prima donna image. What I hadn't guessed was how very trusting and gentle and...childlike you can be."

Vera smiled pleasantly. "All performers are children, Caroline. I often think it's a prerequisite." Her eyes misted over for a minute. "I've thrown my fair share of tantrums, it's true...but only during rehearsals, if things weren't going smoothly. I never yelled at your father, or you either, for that matter." Then Vera returned to the present and smiled. "I'm a ruthless perfectionist about music, my dear, but otherwise I'm rather docile and easy to get along with."

"Perhaps," Caroline said gently, "that's because nothing else meant that much to you."

Vera laughed softly. "Before we had that little chat on your first night here, I'd have argued that with you. I loved your father deeply, Caroline, and I've always loved you. But you're right. Up until my retirement, music meant everything to me. It came first in all my thoughts and decisions, which is why I was able to succeed and stay at the top all those years. Absolute dedication is the only way to survive in professional music. Everything else has to play second fiddle."

"Did you plan that awful pun," Caroline accused, laughing.

"No," Vera said, and they both grinned impishly.

The household intercom buzzed, interrupting their moment of companionship, and Vera picked up the receiver. "Yes?" She listened for a few moments, then turned to Caroline. "Victor says the Spanish doctor is on the phone, and John wants you to translate the lab results."

"Tell them I'll be right down," she requested, already on her feet and moving toward the door.

Chapter 12

After checking a few of the medical terms in a Spanish-English dictionary, Caroline provided a full translation of what the doctor reported. John was satisfied with the results, explaining that Vera was suffering from nothing more than a case of salmonella. He also granted Vera permission to join them at table that evening, provided she had nothing but soft-boiled eggs and dry toast.

Victor smiled at the restricted menu. "She won't like that at all," he said.

"It'll be difficult for her to cheat with her doctor seated across from her," John replied, winking at Caroline.

Nodding, Victor responded, "If anyone can find a way, Vera will. By the way," he said, turning to Caroline, "I won't be needing the car today. Why don't I have Alejandro drive you two over to Barcelona for a couple of hours' sightseeing?"

"That's a great idea," Caroline said, "but let's not bother Alejandro. We can manage by ourselves."

"Don't worry about being a bother, that's what Alejandro is paid to do," Victor reasoned. "Besides, if you want to get out and take a closer look at something or visit a museum, you'll never find a parking space. It will be easier if you have a driver who can stay with the car, especially if it's parked illegally!"

Much as she disliked the idea of having Alejandro around, Caroline couldn't think of a discreet way out of it. She agreed, finally, and she and John were in Victor's Peugeot half an hour later, with the silent enigmatic Alejandro at the wheel.

"An afternoon isn't nearly enough time," she said to John as the car wound down the hill to Badalona and out onto the highway. "But at least you'll get a little of the flavor of the city."

John grinned. "As long as I'm with you, that's all that counts," he said gallantly.

"I think you'll really enjoy the old quarter of Barcelona. Locals usually just refer to it as *la ciudad*, and it dates back to the founding of the city before the time of Christ. But we'll have to walk, a car this size wouldn't make it through the narrow winding streets."

"Then Victor was right to suggest a driver," John replied.

She didn't say anything to that. "Gaudí's surrealistic architecture is also very interesting, but I don't think we should bother to do more than drive past.... There's just no time."

"That's all right, Caroline. Really."

"Then there's the *Rambla*, the Palace of the Counts of Barcelona, the Beaux Arts Museum with its fabulous Gothic and Roman works of art...."

"Hold on a second," John interrupted, laughing. "You're going to wear me out! First you take me on that death-defying climb to the cove, and now you're going to walk my legs into stumps!"

"Obviously, you're not a very keen tourist," she teased.

He smiled. "I'm an Englishman, Caroline. There's only one place worth seeing, and that's England."

"Or Italy," she commented. "I've never understood the fascination Italy holds for the English."

"It's warm and sunny," he replied, smiling.

The outskirts of the city came into view, and soon they were driving down the beautiful *Rambla*, a tree-lined avenue with tables and umbrellas dotting the sidewalks. It was here that people paused in their day to have a snack or a glass of *sangría* while watching the pedestrians saunter by. The boulevard divided the old section of the city and led directly to the port, a heavily trafficked harbor.

Soon the famous cathedral, dedicated to Saint Eulalia, came into view, and Caroline explained how it had been built in 1298 on the site of what was once a Roman temple, later a Moorish mosque and finally an early Christian church. Alejandro pulled over to the curb, and John and Caroline got out of the car. "This way," she said, linking her arm through his and leading him toward a side street.

"I see what you mean about no cars," he said. "There's hardly enough space for people."

"It's fascinating to come down here. The musty old shops are a delight, and I love to observe the people who live in this quarter. Many of them would make intriguing portrait studies."

John looked up at the canyonlike ancient structures. "Are those apartments up there, over the shops?"

"Yes, but you wouldn't want to live here. There's no running water or plumbing, and the buildings are too old to renovate, even if someone wanted to."

"But why would anyone live here then?" John asked.

She paused in front of a used-and-rare bookstore, browsing through the books in the cracked wooden box outside to see if there were any volumes on art. Finding none, she turned to John. "Why do poor people live in tenements and ugly council houses? Because they have to. . . . If you don't have enough money to buy an apartment, then you live where the rent is cheap."

"I understand that," he said gravely, "but no running water?"

"We don't have a refrigerator in Hampstead, and many people would think that's a terrible hardship," she replied.

He snorted. "But mother goes to the market every day, so we don't need a refrigerator. It would be a waste of money."

"Not if you were used to it," she countered. "Can you imagine my mother living without all her American comforts?"

"Not for a second," he answered, laughing. "I suppose you're right—it's all a question of what one's accustomed to."

As they strolled along, Caroline pointed out the public bathhouse, with the water pumps in the street, and a cobblestoned lane crowded with shoppers and vendors. The sound of music came from the apartments and shops, and the smells of different tantalizing foods filled the air. She tugged John over to one food vendor, and taking a tissue-thin piece of waxed paper, half wrapped a round, deep-fried morsel and handed it to John. "Taste it," she urged.

"Looks like an onion ring," he said, taking a bite. "It's delicious—what is it?"

"Batter-fried squid," she said, helping herself to one and smiling at the vendor, who nodded pleasantly.

John swallowed hard, his eyes widening with horror. "Squid?"

Caroline laughed. "Don't be squeamish. You just said how good it was."

He held out a palmful of coins and the vendor took what he needed. Then they walked a little farther until Caroline squealed happily and ran to another cart. *"Empanadillas!* Oh, John, you must try one!" Turning to the vendor, she asked in Spanish, "Are they ham or tuna?"

"Before you give me one," John said cautiously, "maybe you should tell me what it is."

"Pastry turnovers with either ham or tuna stuffing."

"You're quite sure?"

"Absolutely," she answered, laughing. "Have I ever lied to you?"

"No," he said slowly, "but you didn't tell me what I was eating until after I asked you."

They'd reached a point in the street where the buildings had sagged so close together that the sun couldn't penetrate the spaces between them. Walking along a shady portion of the sidewalk, they peered into the window of an antique shop. When they straightened and turned, John was nearly knocked down by a lurching man staggering past them.

"Why the devil don't you—" the man started to say.

"Patrick!" Caroline said, not quite able to believe her eyes. He was so drunk he could hardly stand, and the whites of his eyes were bloodshot.

"Well, well...if it isn't the happy tourists," Patrick slurred. "Slumming, Caroline?"

She bristled, irritated by his manner. "At least I'm sober," she replied tersely.

Pat laughed raucously. "Shocked, Caroline?"

"Come on, John, let's get out of here," was her only reply.

AFTER SUPPER THAT EVENING, Victor entertained them with anecdotes from his life as an art dealer. No mention had been made about Patrick's absence from the table, and no explanation was offered. Vera had taken care to look especially lovely, though she had used too much rouge to make herself seem healthier.

Caroline only half listened as Victor spoke. Her mind kept drifting back to Pat's strange behavior. Why on earth had he felt compelled to get drunk. It seemed out of character for him, at least at odds with the impression of him in Caroline's mind.

"I suppose you also have to worry about crooks trying to pass off forgeries," John was saying to Victor.

"Oh, of course! But I'm very careful. If I'm at all in doubt, I consult an expert to authenticate the work. Some very clever swindles have happened in the art world."

"You really should write a book, Victor," Vera said,

then turned to John. "Now then, young man. Before time gets away from us and you're off home, I want to invite you to come back whenever you like. Spend your holidays here, if you wish. . . . I'm sure Caroline would love to have more time to show you the sights."

"Thank you, Mrs. O'Flaherty. I'll certainly consider it," he answered amiably.

"Well, shall we have a brandy?" Victor asked, then rose and moved to the bar. "Caroline? You've been very quiet this evening."

"Yes, please, Victor. And you're right, I'm afraid I haven't been very good company tonight." She felt terrible about not being a better hostess to John, but she just couldn't keep her thoughts away from Patrick. Something must have happened this morning to upset him, and it might conceivably have something to do with her. She had gone over her behavior repeatedly during the afternoon, but could think of nothing that would have angered him.

"Perhaps you're tired," John offered sympathetically, breaking into her troubled thoughts. "I doubt that you're accustomed to all the climbing and walking we did today—particularly not in the hot sun," he added.

"Did you take John for a long walk?" Victor asked, handing her a brandy snifter partially filled with the aromatic amber liquid.

Caroline recognized the snifter as part of a set her father had had a local manufacturer design. The Spanish were excellent glassmakers, though few foreigners realized it. "Yes," she answered, "I dared him to come down to the cove with me."

"What cove, dear?" Vera asked, accepting her drink from her husband.

"There's one at the base of the almond grove, down a very steep path," Caroline explained.

"I don't think I've ever seen it," Vera remarked.

"It's practically a vertical climb, Mrs. O'Flaherty. You may want to skip that particular scenic attraction."

"It sounds dangerous," Victor said flatly. Then he smiled cordially. "But of course, now that you've been there, there's no reason to return."

"Perhaps, but it's always been one of my favorite places," Caroline replied. "It's so peaceful and isolated."

John and Victor drifted into a conversation about the high cost of medical care, whether National Health was a success in England, and the surprise election of a woman as prime minister. Caroline was glad to see that the two men had so much to discuss and noted that Vera was also pleased. She was quite amused to see how deftly her mother had accepted a brandy without John noticing. Obviously, John was having entirely too good a time to have objected.

The evening wore on, and Caroline tried to participate in the discussions whenever she could. But her mind kept drifting back to Pat's sudden dislike of her.

Finally they decided to call it a night and retire. Her mother, Victor and John went upstairs, saying their good-nights as they left, and Caroline walked down the hallway to her own room. She hesitated before the door and realized she was too wound up to go to bed right then. Turning, she retraced her steps and headed for the kitchen.

Señora Mendez was just hanging up the dish towel,

and young Consuelo had fallen asleep at the table with her head on her hands. "Is there a flashlight in here?" Caroline asked in a whisper.

The woman nodded and pulled one out of a drawer, handing it to Caroline. *"Gracias,"* Caroline said, and borrowing a shawl from a peg near the back door, she let herself out into the nearly black night. The air was crisp and cool as it usually was at night in that part of Spain. The moon was only a sliver, and the stars seemed close enough to be plucked from the sky.

Caroline began to walk leisurely, aimlessly, letting her thoughts go where they would. She had no concept of how much time had passed since she left the house, but when she realized she was near the almond grove, she knew she'd been walking for at least a half hour. Even with the flashlight she didn't want to risk going into the small wood at night, so instead she walked to the edge of the promontory.

When she reached the rim, she switched off the light and sat down on a flat boulder nearby. In the distance she could see a yacht moored, its lights reflected by the dark water. From where she was, Caroline could only dimly make out the cove to her left. But the night was so quiet she could hear the sea's soft lapping even from that height above it.

Suddenly she thought she heard the sound of oars cutting into the water. It was a rhythmic sound, out of tempo with the gentle lapping of the waves. Stretching cautiously across the large rock, Caroline saw a dinghy approaching the shore. The two men in it were illuminated by the light of a battery-operated lantern, which was switched off, then on, then off again. Caroline was mystified. They seemed to be signaling someone, yet who would be down there at this hour? When the small boat reached the shore, one of the men held the lantern; the other pulled the dinghy onto the sand.

Almost immediately a dull light illuminated a rectangular patch of sand. Completely taken aback, Caroline wondered if she was imagining things. She didn't recognize either of the two men, but shortly thereafter a small wiry man joined them, and she thought she detected something familiar about him. He gestured to them, and the three walked out of her view, beneath the cliff. Then the third man returned, and Caroline could not mistake the build or carriage of the man on the beach below her. "Alejandro!" she gasped to herself.

"What are you doing here, alone at this hour of the night!"

Frightened by the unexpected voice, Caroline started and jumped to her feet, "Patrick!"

"I asked you a question, Caroline. Why are you here?"

Still rather shocked by the scene below, Caroline felt nervous faced with his demanding manner. "I don't think it's any of your business," she managed to stutter.

He came toward her slowly, his hands clenched into fists as if he were about to strike her. "Are you following me? Is that why you turn up wherever I go?"

Anger made his Irish brogue even more pronounced, and Caroline realized that he was serious. He actually thought she might have nothing better to do than wonder where he was. "You know, you really have a stupendous ego, Pat. Why should I care where you are?"

"I think you know the answer to that," he muttered in a low, almost threatening voice. He took another step toward her and placed his hands on her arms. "Ever since you came here, nothing's been the same. What's your game, Caroline?"

"Take your hands off me," she answered, feeling a mounting fear. The moonlight played eerily across his strong features, making him look monstrous, and his brows were arched over his hazel eyes in a way that seemed demoniacal.

"I want to know what's going on," he said in a strange voice. "Victor has instructed me to stop all construction and work here. He told me early this morning, after you'd been up with him late last night. What did you tell him, Caroline?"

"Tell him! I didn't have a chance to get a word in edgewise," she protested genuinely. She was afraid of Patrick, afraid that he was still inebriated and unable to think clearly.

"You must have," Pat snarled. "Up until you arrived, he wanted this place rebuilt quickly. He told me the vineyards and winery had to be restored swiftly, that he wanted to assure Vera of an independent income as fast as possible. Now his instructions are to come to a dead halt. You may think that living here as a child gives you certain rights, but it's *my* knowledge and sweat that will make Foxdale successful. You've only taken from this estate, Caroline; I've given to it, worked for it. This place is in my blood now, and if the land could speak, it would tell you whose toil it respects!"

"You're talking gibberish," Caroline said. "Let go of me, Pat," she implored, stepping backward.

Before she realized what was happening, she felt the land beneath her feet begin to give way. All she could

hear was a sick crunching, like the sound of a tooth being pulled from its socket.

"Caroline!"

She hardly heard the voice calling her name. Caroline
only knew she was losing her footing. She was slipping . . . sliding down the side of the rocky promontory.

Chapter 13

"But how in the world did it happen?" Vera demanded, her dark eyes troubled as she gazed down at Caroline.

John was bending over Caroline, dabbing iodine on the cuts and scrapes on her arms and legs. "Mrs. O'Flaherty, would you get a warm blanket to wrap around her?"

"Of course," she said, and left the room.

"You're very lucky," John said, shaking his head. "You could have been killed! And here you are, not even a scratch on your face."

She tried to smile but couldn't. "The rest of me is making up for that," she said. "My arms feel as if they'd been pulled out of their sockets." Still in shock, she was unable to control the slight trembling of her body.

Victor had seated himself on the divan, across from where John had placed Caroline in the wingback chair. His cold blue eyes seemed far away even though he was looking directly at her. "You say you went for a stroll, ran into Patrick, and then this accident occurred," he reiterated. "Why were you so close to the edge, Caroline?" He looked up as Vera reentered the room and placed the comforter around her daughter. "For that matter," Victor concluded, "you should know better than to be walking that far afield late at night!"

John put the cap back on the bottle, remarking, "That should prevent infection. I only wish you'd told me you were going out—I'd have come with you."

"I wanted to be by myself, Johnnie. I just happened to go a lot farther than I'd realized, and. . . ."

"Well, thank heaven Patrick was nearby," Vera said, sitting next to her husband.

Caroline looked down at the rug, to hide the expression of doubt on her face. The incident had happened so quickly that she wasn't sure whether she'd fallen or been pushed. But if Patrick *had* pushed her, why did he change his mind and save her by pulling her back onto solid ground? He could have just let her drop, and everyone would have assumed it was a fatal accident, that she'd been unable to see where she was going.

"Would you like a sedative?" John asked her.

Temporarily shaken out of her reverie, she replied, "No, I'm fine now."

"Where is Pat, by the way?" Victor scowled as he glanced around the living room. "Didn't he come in with us?"

"I don't know," John answered. "I heard him calling my name, saying that Caroline had been hurt. When I looked out my window and saw him carrying her, I threw on my robe and came right down."

"That must have been about the time I opened the door to see what all the noise was about," Victor said. "I saw you rushing out and came after you to find out what was wrong."

"Pat carried her in here," John said, "and I haven't seen him since."

As the three of them talked about what had happened, Caroline remained silent. She was still desperately curious to learn why those men had rowed to the cove and what Alejandro had been doing there. But she somehow sensed that any questions might upset Victor and Vera—or prove dangerous for *her*. Whatever the chauffeur was up to, it was obviously covert.

When Caroline was young, there had been a great deal of illegal activity along the shores near Badalona. Smugglers brought in contraband liquor and cigarettes, and who knew what else. She could still remember how her father used to chuckle about Scotch whiskey and English cigarettes being almost as cheap in Spain as in England.

Could that sort of thing still be going on, she wondered? And if it was, would Alejandro be mixed up in it? There would be virtually no way for bulky heavy cartons to be brought up the steep path from the cove. And it would be even more difficult to transport the contraband into town. But perhaps the contraband wasn't meant to be moved. Maybe Alejandro was allowing the cove to be used as a temporary hideout for the smugglers.

She wished she'd been able to see everything that had transpired down there! Patrick had interrupted her before she could watch the dinghy being unloaded. Then it occurred to her that one of the three men might have seen her struggling with Patrick. The thought chilled her, and she was glad when John's voice brought her back to reality.

"I think you'd better go to bed now," he said, his brow furrowed with worry. "You've had quite enough for one day."

Caroline rose unsteadily, even with John's aid. "I suppose you're right."

Vera came over and embraced her daughter warmly. "I'm only thankful that you're all right," she said genuinely. "I think we should all try to get some rest. Coming, Victor?"

"Not just yet, dear. I think I'll read in the study for a while. With all this excitement I'm not at all tired. You go ahead. I'll be up in a little while."

Caroline stiffly made her way across the room. John carefully helped her down the hall, past Victor's study, and opened the door to help her inside her bedroom. "Will you be all right?" he asked. "Maybe I should stay at Foxdale for another couple of days."

"No, I'm fine, Johnnie—just tired. And you should be in Hampstead, where you're really needed."

"Frankly, Caroline, I don't like the idea of that Patrick fellow hanging around. He certainly hasn't made a favorable impression on me today. Oh, I know he saved your life," he said when she tried to interrupt. "But I can certainly see why you took such an instant dislike to him! Surly behavior, drunk, and then wandering around the premises in the middle of the night. . . ."

Caroline was tempted to reply that there was another side to Pat, a sweet, gentle side. But she was worried that it might hurt John's feelings. Besides what *did* she know about Patrick O'Flaherty? She had only seen his better side once, at the *cantina*. The rest of the time they'd either been arguing, or he'd been suspiciously furious with her, like tonight.

She allowed John to kiss her lightly on the cheek as he said good-night, and she climbed into bed the moment he left. Now, more than ever, she believed that something was very wrong at Foxdale. Were Patrick and Alejandro in this together? Or was the servant acting independently?

Pat had spoken to her with such sincerity out on the bluff, that she found it difficult to doubt his devotion to Foxdale. Surely that had been sincere. And then she remembered what he'd said about Victor reversing his instructions about completing the restoration of the estate as quickly as possible. Pat had seemed to feel that she was at the root of this sudden switch. Knowing that she wasn't, Caroline speculated on why Victor had changed his mind.

Perhaps Victor had become suspicious of Alejandro's activities, she thought. But even so, that would be no reason to stop the construction work or clearing the vineyards.

In spite of all the unanswered questions, Caroline began to drift off to sleep. The last thing that entered her mind was the image of the men down at the cove, and of the rectangular shaft of light. Where did that light come from? She knew it wasn't the lantern, because it had shed its own glow. Unless there was a door set into the wall of the cliff, and that was impossible!

IN THE MORNING, long before anyone was stirring in the household, Caroline put on a pair of blue jeans and sneakers and decided to go back to the cove. Though the idea of going anywhere near the spot where she had fallen turned her knees to jelly, she was determined to find some answers to the questions that had plagued her just before she had fallen asleep.

Caroline knew she had not imagined the rectangular light, and it could only mean that there *was* a secret door built into the shale and sandy soil at the base of the bluff. And, if a door was hidden there, it had to lead to something. A storage space carved out of the cliff? A subterranean tunnel? Who had constructed it and why? Whatever the reason, it must have required a lot of determination to keep the construction a secret. And someone must have had a very important reason to have gone to all that trouble, and expense!

The dew was still on the grass as she let herself out of the house. Even though she was certain everyone in the household was still asleep, Caroline had gone out the front door and planned to take the long way around to avoid awakening anyone, especially Alejandro.

The air was light and faintly aromatic with the first stirrings of the earth and shrubbery; the sky was a gray blue, and lavender clouds reflected the sun's arrival on the horizon. Although it was still rather cool, Caroline knew that walking would keep her warm, and she didn't want any encumbrances, such as a jacket, when she reached the edge of the almond grove.

She forced herself to walk at an easy pace, like someone enjoying a morning constitutional, until she was out of sight of the house. Then she began to walk more briskly. It took her almost forty-five minutes to reach the grove, going the long way. The clouds were now wisps of white against a pale cerulean blue, and the sun was rapidly warming up the air. Cautiously, but purposefully, Caroline made her way down steep path, reminding herself over and over that the stone steps were solid and wouldn't give way beneath her.

Finally Caroline reached the damp sandy beach and drew a breath of relief. She strolled over to the spot at the water's edge where she thought the dinghy had been pulled ashore. There were no traces of footprints, much less indentations from the hull of the rowboat. Obviously all suspicious marks had been carefully erased, and the Mediterranean's gentle waves had finished what the men had started.

Caroline hadn't really expected to find any evidence of the boat and the three men, but she had wanted to be sure anyway. Ironically their very thoroughness now convinced her that Alejandro and his cohorts were up to no good. She crouched near the water's edge, still trying to think of what they might be smuggling. Then an awful thought crossed her mind. They might be trafficking in narcotics. Not only was it highly profitable, but she'd heard that some drugs didn't take up very much space and were easily transportable.

She turned her back to the sun and scanned the side of the cliff, determined to find their hiding place. Rocks jutted from the sand and shale, and it was difficult to make out anything in the jumble until she remembered a trick she had learned at art school. She cupped her palm and fingers into a spyglass shape, which eliminated any optical distractions and offered a better examination.

Methodically, Caroline searched one side of the cliff wall and then the other, straining to find anything that might even suggest that the rock face had been tampered with. But, in the end, she gave up. Whoever had built the door had done it expertly. There was no sign that anything manmade had been built into the earth and rocks.

"What did you expect to find," she said to herself dryly. "Hinges and a knob?"

She sat down on the sand and tried to think of some other means of locating the hidden door. Discouraged by her failure, she began to think the whole idea of a storage room inside the cliff was ridiculous; it was just too far-fetched, like something out of "Ali Baba and the Forty Thieves." Wryly, she wondered if it would do any good to go up to the wall and say, "Open sesame."

She had to admit that the odds were against her theory. Even in Spain, the cost of labor would be prohibitive to build such a cave. Caroline strongly doubted that someone like Alejandro—even if he were a drug smuggler—could have found the money needed to build it. Even wealthy Victor could not have afforded it. And how could someone undertake such a massive project without being detected? She started to feel that she might be the victim of an overactive imagination. Then she remembered the strange patch of light. She knew that she had seen it and just couldn't dismiss it that easily, however foolish the idea of a storage room might seem.

It occurred to her fleetingly that it might be wise to go the Spanish police and tell them what she'd observed. But without any proof, she guessed they'd only laugh at her.

Caroline heard a slight scraping sound and then a dull thud and looked up quickly. Her emotions were fragmented as she saw Patrick coming toward her. "Now who's following whom?" she asked with mild sarcasm.

His lopsided grin was sheepish. "I saw you from my room in the new wing. I . . . well, I wanted to be alone with you when I apologized for yesterday."

"You saved my life last night, Pat. . . . Why should you

feel as if you have to apologize for anything?" Her voice was indifferent, as if there was nothing left for either of them to say to each other.

Pat sat down next to her, a forlorn expression in his hazel eyes. "I'm afraid my temper gets away from me sometimes," he said slowly. "I was rude to you and Dr. Clarke in Barcelona, and there was no excuse for my behavior last night. I had no right to accuse you of being up to something."

"You're right on all points," she agreed. Though she was glad to know that Pat was the sort of man who was capable of admitting that he was wrong, she still wasn't about to capitulate with total forgiveness and suggest a fresh beginning.

Pat looked at her steadily for a moment, then glanced away. "Something happened yesterday morning that upset me terribly," he said softly. "It wasn't just Victor's instructions to stop work on the estate; it was something I don't wish to discuss right now. I jumped to the conclusion that you were behind the whole thing and took it out on you. I'm very genuinely sorry, Caroline. I should have known that my conversation with Victor had nothing to do with you, that you knew nothing about it."

"Why were you at the cliffs last night?" Caroline tried to keep her voice calm, but there was still some doubt in her mind about Pat. For all she knew, he might be involved with Alejandro—or he might have meant to back her over the edge of the cliff.

He snorted under his breath. "I was walking off the excesses of my afternoon in town. I frequently walk around the grounds at night, to think things through or try to solve an engineering problem before the next day's work. But when I saw you there, too, it sparked off my worst suspicions. I actually thought you were spying on me." He leaned forward slightly, tucking his head lower than hers and looking up her. "Forgiven? Can we be friends again?"

"Did you mean to harm me last night, Pat? Please tell me the truth, for my own sake, as well as yours. It's one thing to have a bad temper and quite another to have a streak of violence."

"I swear to you nothing could have been farther from my mind!" He twisted around and gazed at her earnestly as he spoke, shock and amazement written on his face. "I don't know what I'd do if anything happened to you, Caroline! I...well, I've come to be quite fond of you. But even if I hadn't, I'm not a violent man and never have been."

"Not even when you've had too much to drink?"

"No, never. And I want you to know it's a rare day indeed that Patrick O'Flaherty goes off on a binge. I only indulge myself when I'm feeling concerned."

"That's the worst time, don't you think?" She couldn't help smiling at the contradiction of his logic, yet she believed him. He just wasn't the type to become physically abusive, she felt sure of that. Presumably, with both of them so close to the edge, the ground had simply given way under their weight.

"You're probably right," Pat said in response to her question. "But I've never struck a man who didn't hit me first, and I'm incapable of harming a woman."

"All right, Pat," she answered, a forgiving look in her dark brown eyes as she put out her right hand. "Friends again."

He grinned broadly, taking the hand she offered. "'Tis a happy man you're making me, Caroline!"

They were silent for a few moments, both deep in their own private thoughts as they watched the sun's dancing reflections on the sea. "Do you come down to this cove often?" Caroline finally asked.

Pat shook his head. "No, not really. I'm usually too busy. Look at how much work's been accomplished in the past six weeks—there's not much time for swimming or any other recreation. Of course, now that everything is at a standstill, I suppose I'll have some time on my hands."

Caroline leaned back, wrapping her arms around her knees. "Does Alejandro ever help you with your work?" she asked, then added casually, "He's such a strange man, even a bit frightening sometimes."

Pat laughed. "Since I don't know sign language, I hardly know the man at all. If he weren't so accursedly ugly, I don't think you'd be afraid of him."

"Perhaps," she conceded. "Yet even without that awful scar, he has such a sinister look in his eyes whenever I see him."

"Are you sure that's what it is? Couldn't it be fear of rejection? He's very different when he's with Victor—much less tense. I think he worships my uncle."

"Has he been with Victor for a long time?" Caroline asked.

Pat squinted as he tried to remember. "No, I don't think so, not like the proverbial old family servant, if that's what you mean. If I recall correctly, Victor hired him about seven or eight years ago. And, being the man he is," Pat added, an admiring look on his face, "Victor immediately learned sign language. Victor's a strange man until you get to know him. He throws himself into everything he does, almost to the point of becoming obsessed. There don't seem to be any grays in his world, only blacks and whites. He'll either like a man or he'll hate him. There's no middle ground."

"Is he that way about art, too?"

Pat laughed, nodding. "He's worse. It's everything to him."

"Yes, I noticed that," Caroline said, almost to herself. "He was telling me a little bit about his attitude toward art, and toward my mother, on Sunday night after you and I got back from Badalona. It seemed to me that he's turned his existence into a kind of museum or shrine, and that he allows only beautiful and perfect things around him."

"Perhaps," Pat concurred reluctantly. "But then there's Alejandro—he certainly doesn't fit into what you've described."

"No, I guess not."

"Why are you curious about Alejandro, by the way?"

"Oh...no special reason," she fibbed. She wanted desperately to confide in Pat, to tell him what she had witnessed last night, but she didn't feel that the time was right. Whatever was going on at Foxdale, she needed more evidence before discussing it...with anyone.

"Let's go back to the house," she said, changing the subject. "I'm famished, aren't you?"

Chapter 14

John was coming downstairs as Pat and Caroline entered the house, laughing quietly and talking softly so they wouldn't disturb anyone else. Caroline had almost forgotten that John was there, but the slight frown on his face as he watched them come inside didn't escape her.

"Good morning, Dr. Clarke," Patrick said cheerfully.

"We've been for a long walk," Caroline added. "You should have come with us," she said, hoping to erase the look of disapproval on John's face.

"To the cove, I suppose," he replied as he reached them.

Caroline didn't doubt for a moment that John was jealous and wondering if Pat perhaps meant more to her than she would admit. It seemed so strange to think of Johnnie being jealous of her. Fortunately, Pat spared her from having to tell the truth in answer to John's question.

"We're on our way for a spot of breakfast in the kitchen, Dr. Clarke. Won't you join us? I'd also like to say I'm sorry for my rudeness to you yesterday. I was in a foul mood, I'm afraid, though I know that's no excuse." Pat smiled charmingly from John to Caroline.

"No need to apologize," John remarked, but it was evident that he still didn't think much of Pat's behavior.

"There was a little more to it than that," Caroline interjected, "but Pat's explained everything and apologized."

"I see," John said. There was a note of uncertainty in his voice, but he went with them toward the kitchen nonetheless.

Pat whispered to Caroline, "Shall I ask Mrs. Mendez to serve in the dining room?"

"Why?"

"Well, your friend is a doctor, after all."

Caroline smiled. "He's not that kind of a doctor," she whispered back.

"What's that?" John asked, turning to look at them.

"Nothing, Johnnie. Pat was worried that you'd take offense at eating in the kitchen, that's all."

They filed in, greeting Consuelo and the cook, and by the time breakfast was over, John was obviously in a far better mood. He no longer seemed so wary of Patrick and had adopted a possessive attitude toward Caroline, talking about when she returned to Hampstead and resumed her studies. "She's very talented, you know," he said to Pat.

"I'm sure she is," he responded. "I'd like to see some of your work one day," Pat said to her.

"Well, next time you're in England, you must come up for dinner," John said, almost cordially, "I'm sure Caroline will be delighted to show you her portfolio."

Caroline smiled. "You make me sound like a precocious child anxious to show her scrapbook." She sipped her coffee, then said, "Well, we'll see how good I am when it's time to get a job."

John looked at her quickly. "You're not still thinking of a career, are you?"

"Why, of course," she said. "I haven't been going to school for my own amusement, Johnnie."

He frowned slightly. "Perhaps we should discuss this once you're home again."

Patrick raised one eyebrow curiously. "Isn't this your home now, Caroline?"

Realizing that the conversation was getting out of hand and that there was an undercurrent of friction between the two men, Caroline looked at her watch pointedly. "Good heavens! It's almost nine o'clock! You'll miss your plane, John, if we don't leave soon."

"I'm all packed, Caroline," John said easily. "The only thing I want to do is have another look at your mother before I leave. That, and say thank you to both your mother and Mr. O'Flaherty."

"We can do that for you," Pat said. "What time's your flight?"

"Check-in time is ten o'clock," Caroline interrupted. "That's just about the time mother's trying to pry her eyes open. Pat's right, John, we'll have to say your good-byes for you. They'll understand."

Patrick leaned back in his chair, tilting it on its rear legs. "It's strange that Victor isn't up and about, though. He's usually an early riser."

"Perhaps he's in his study," Caroline offered.

"Do I have time for another cup of coffee?" John asked.

"Go ahead," she answered. "I'll only be a few moments; I've got to get out of these clothes and into something proper." She rose from the table and walked quickly to her room, already deciding what she would put on. She was going to miss having John around. In the brief period he'd been at Foxdale, it had almost been like being back in England. She had been secure in the knowledge that he was nearby should she need him.

She changed quickly and as she was returning from her room to fetch John, she noted that Victor's study door wasn't fully closed. She was about to pull it shut then decided to ignore it. Her primary concern now was to get Johnnie to the airport on time.

John and Pat were standing in the front hall, and John was looking at his watch impatiently.

"Shall we go?" Caroline smiled, hoping that he wasn't too angry with her.

"You look lovely," Pat said, beaming.

"Thank you," she murmured, opening the front door while John picked up his overnight bag.

"Well, thanks again," John said hurriedly. "Call us up if you get to London."

Moments later they were in the car with Alejandro at the wheel, and the time seemed to fly by as they drove to the airport. Caroline didn't like the idea of having to go back with the chauffeur all by herself, but didn't see how she could avoid it.

They got to the departure terminal on time, and she went with John to the check-in counter, then to the passenger lounge to wait for his flight to board. They chatted aimlessly, neither of them saying what they wanted to. It was as if they had suddenly become strangers.

It seemed forever to Caroline before the announcement was made in Spanish and English that John's flight was boarding at Gate Eleven. People began to gather up packages and totebags, and a crowd milled toward the gate where a line was forming. She accompanied John until it was his turn to join the other passengers in the roped-in area.

He turned and looked down at her, his gray eyes a little sad. "I wish we could have had more time, Caroline, but I suppose a little is better than none at all. Will you write to me?"

"Of course," she answered, reaching up to embrace him.

He put his arms around her and held her to him tightly, then lowered his face to kiss her. Just as his lips brushed against hers, the ticket taker tapped him on the shoulder, indicating that John was holding up the line.

"I'll miss you," Caroline called. "Give everyone my love and hug them for me!"

John waved, then he was out of sight.

"DID YOUR FRIEND get off all right?" Vera came into the living room wearing a Givenchy pantsuit, looking very much like her usual self.

"Yes, mother," Caroline replied, then explained why John hadn't said good-bye formally.

"Nice young man, dear, but I don't think he's the one for you." Vera moved over to the end table and rearranged the fresh cut flowers in the vase. "He's much too serious. But then, I suppose all doctors are. I'd like to see you marry a man with more verve and spark."

Caroline smiled. "Well, whatever you think of John, he's not greedy. He didn't want to send you a bill for his services, but I told him . . . ."

"Oh, I completely forgot," Vera interrupted. "Victor made out a check for the airfare and what he assumed would be a reasonable sum for a London-to-Badalona house call. Darn! I should have asked Victor to give it to John before he left this morning."

"That'a all right, mother. We can mail it to him."

"I suppose we'll have to," her mother said, mildly irritated. "Victor will be in Barcelona all day, and I don't know where he put the check."

"Perhaps it's in his study," Caroline suggested.

"Of course! Run in and see if there's something on the desk, will you?"

Caroline stood up and walked across the room. When she reached the door, Vera said, "Oh, I forgot to ask how you're feeling this morning."

"A bit stiff and sore, but that's all. I think I looked a lot worse last night than I really was," she said, then left the room.

As she entered the study, Caroline suddenly sensed that she wasn't alone. She felt as if someone was there with her, or perhaps had just left. It was a strange feeling and a silly one, but one she'd experienced before, when she'd used the telephone in Victor's study.

Then she chided herself. Victor was away, and no one else in the house would have reason to be in his study. She was just letting her imagination run away with her again. Caroline moved to the desk, and right on top, just as she'd expected, was a white business-sized envelope with "Dr. John Clarke" written in dark blue ink.

For a second, Caroline could only stare at Victor's handwriting, surprised at all the flourishes he managed to get in so few words. Compared to Victor's handwriting, her own was like printing. Rather amused at his old-fashioned style, she picked up the envelope and started back for the door. Then she stopped. Something was wrong with the room. Hesitantly, she turned and surveyed the walls.

The Bruegal was gone. In its place was a much smaller oil painting of comparatively little value. She knew that Victor liked to rotate the pictures in the house, but it suddenly occurred to her that not one of the pictures she'd seen when she first arrived at Foxdale, including the Signac from her bedroom, had been hung elsewhere. Each and every painting had been substituted for an unknown work and never seen again. She glanced around a second time to see if the original paintings were stacked anywhere, but they weren't. Hadn't her mother said the attic was still boarded up? If the paintings weren't up there, and they weren't here... where were they? She knew that Victor couldn't have sold the copies to anyone, he was too respectable and reputable to try to pass off copies on his clients.

Confused, Caroline pulled the study door closed behind her. She mulled over the mystery as she walked back across the hall to the living room. Then she remembered something she had heard at school as a child, and the pieces began to fall into place. Before she could put the whole puzzle together, she had arrived back at the living room. "Here's the check," she said to her mother as she reentered the room.

"Good. That's a relief," said Vera as she took the envelope from her daughter.

"Mother...how did Victor get to Barcelona this morning?"

"I suppose Alejandro drove him. Why?"

Caroline shook her head. "No, Alejandro was with me. He drove us to the airport, then took me home. There wouldn't have been time for him to have returned here to pick up Victor and still be back at the airport to collect me."

"Well, dear, then I suppose Victor called a taxi. Wasn't it sweet of him to let you have the car even though he needed it."

Caroline moved to the windows overlooking the front lawn. She could just see a corner of the rose garden from where she stood. The rose garden, where the earth trembled. "Would you mind if I didn't join you for lunch today?"

"Well, yes, I'd mind, dear...but if you have something to do...."

"I want to go into Badalona," Caroline said softly. "I'll walk, though. It'll do me good."

"Shall I ask Mrs. Mendez to keep something warm for you?"

Shaking her head, Caroline answered, "Thanks, but I'll grab a bite in town. I should be back around midafternoon.

"All right, dear. I suppose I could catch up on my reading while you're gone. I'm terribly overdue in returning an American book to the library. They're so sweet to me there, always letting me know when they get in a new title in English."

"Yes, I remember how nice and helpful the people at the library were when I was trying to learn Spanish." She kissed Vera on the cheek. Then she picked up her handbag and left the house.

The sun was hot as she started down the hill toward town, and there were very few trees to protect her against it. Despite the oppressive heat, her mind rapidly turned over and over the details of what had happened since she'd arrived at Foxdale. It wasn't just the hidden door in the side of the cliff that was bothering her, or even Alejandro's assignation with those two men. There was more. Much more.

Then she remembered her conversation with Patrick early that morning, how she had compared Victor's world to a museum and a shrine. That was her clue, she was sure of it. Somehow that was connected to all the little mysteries that surrounded her—the episode at the cove, Victor's decision to stop further work on the estate, the missing copies.... She didn't know exactly how yet, but she hoped she would find out either at the Town Clerk's office in Badalona or at the library.

By the time she reached town, her mind was racing with possibilities. She entered the Town Hall, grateful that the high ceilings kept the building cool, and asked if they kept records of all the construction projects that had been undertaken in the area.

"*Sí, señorita*," the clerk answered amiably. "Which building did you have in mind?"

"Foxdale," she replied, then realized he wouldn't understand the English translation and added, "Valle de Zorro."

The clerk pursed his lips, then excused himself. When he returned, he shrugged and shook his head. "Our records go back to the seventeenth century, *señorita*. Remodeling is, however, usually recorded."

"No, what I need to know is the way the house looked when it was originally built, in the first century," Caroline explained.

"*Ay no, señorita*. That we don't have," he said ruefully. "Have you gone to Barcelona, to the Archaeological

Museum, or to the Beaux Arts of Catalán? They might have primitive paintings of the estate or perhaps even a scale model. It is one of the oldest sites in this part of the country, and they may have something."

Caroline thanked him and went back outside, deliberating whether or not to go into Barcelona at once. Somewhere there was the information she needed—information that would put her mind at rest. She opened her purse to see how much money she had with her and found she had more than enough for the train fare and lunch. It was settled, then. She headed down the narrow street toward the sea, where the railroad station was located.

Later, when the train came to a halt in the huge station in Barcelona, Caroline moved swiftly with the crowd to the exit and hailed a taxi. She was glad it was not yet time for the siesta, or her task might have been much more difficult.

The cab pulled up in front of the museum, and Caroline ran up the broad stairs of the ornately decorated building. Moments later, having explained to the curator what she was seeking, he asked her to accompany him into the archives.

"What is stored here," he explained, "is priceless beyond measure. These records and maps date back to ancient times and cannot be put on display."

"I understand," she said, walking quickly to keep up with him. "Are there any diagrams or paintings of the Roman sites?"

"A few," he said, not too encouragingly. "The period you're interested in . . . ." His hands went up as if in surrender. "Well, we'll see what there is. That long ago, only the very wealthy would have commissioned such things."

They went down a wide room with tables and shelves lined with musty tomes. "Many of our treasures are restored here," the curator said. "Some of them are also ruined," he added with a little shrug.

Caroline was too anxious to see if the museum had what she wanted to be amused by his dry humor. He stopped in front of a vault at least eight feet high. "If we have it, it would be in here," he said, pulling open the mammoth metal door.

They entered the almost cold chamber, and the curator went directly to a card index file while Caroline looked around her. Scrolls were filed in neat cubbyholes all along one side of the vault, and wooden boxes housed their secrets along the other side.

"First century, Badalona," the man was saying to himself. "What is the name of the estate again, please?"

"Valle de Zorro," she answered, hardly daring to breathe.

He flipped through a few more cards, his lips moving as he read off the headings to himself. "Ah, here! This should prove helpful."

Caroline watched as he pulled a stepladder over to the shelves holding the scrolls and climbed to the top row. When he came down, he was holding a piece of parchment with the utmost care. He carefully spread it open on a table in the center of the room. "You will not touch this, please—it's too risky. I will hold it for you."

She looked down and could hardly believe her eyes. Before her was a drawing of what Foxdale must have looked like when its first owner, a Roman nobleman, had built it. It had been much, much smaller then, obviously the other rooms had been added over the centuries.

"Is this what you require?" the curator asked.

Nodding, Caroline answered, "I think so. What are these lines down here?" she asked.

"That's the same thing the other foreigner asked. I remember it now."

She looked up. "Foreigner?"

"Yes, I had forgotten until you asked also. A man with strange blue eyes came here about two years ago, maybe more. He seemed very interested in this Roman estate."

"Really?" she said, trying to appear calm.

"When I told him that this was the underground passage to the sea, that there was a vast hiding place beneath the original house, he became very excited."

"I can imagine," Caroline replied. "And this—what does this drawing represent?"

"It's the way to the underground chamber from inside the house," he replied. "See? Here, this room has a connecting wall to the tunnel."

Caroline studied the drawings carefully. They were primitive, but she was beginning to be able to read them. If she was right, the connecting wall today would be in Victor's den. Victor, with his cold blue eyes.

Chapter 15

Caroline made one more stop before returning to Badalona. She went to the Museum of Modern Art which housed paintings from the late eighteenth century by artists of all nationalities. To her surprise, the director of the museum had not heard of any thefts of major works from any of the other museums in Europe.

She felt deflated by the news and realized that the director must have thought her question very odd. But it had been worth a try. From her studies Caroline knew that there was an international network of communication among museum curators, art galleries and dealers. The moment a painting was stolen, they were all alerted to be on the lookout for it, in case an amateur tried to sell it outside the country from which it had been stolen. It was a good system—so good that the director of the Barcelona Museum of Modern Art was guaranteed to hear of any art thefts. . . . But he had heard nothing.

During the train ride back to Badalona, Caroline tried

to make sense of what she had learned, but none of the pieces seemed to fit into the puzzle she thought she had neatly solved. If Victor had been dealing in stolen works of art, then there had to be reports of the missing paintings. Though she clearly recalled him saying that there had been some very clever swindles, certainly his had to be the smartest of them all.

How could he arrange for a work to be stolen, without theft being detected? Yet they must be original works of art. It was inconceivable to Caroline that he was managing to sell forgeries to anyone who was a serious collector. No, people who were willing to spend thousands—sometimes hundreds of thousands—on one painting would be more than willing to spend a bit more to make sure the work was authentic before they made the purchase. It just didn't add up. Victor had to be dealing with the originals... yet none of them was missing.

But at least she now understood the mystery of the hidden door at the foot of the cliff. As the curator had explained to her, Caesar's armies had invaded and conquered most of Spain in the first century B.C. But the native people had not been docile under their foreign lords. As a consequence the Romans who stayed in Spain after the conquest were careful to fortify their estates—and constructed elaborate hiding places. If the local people weren't enough of a threat, the curator had gone on to tell her, there was always the unstable political climate in Rome. Lands granted for bravery by one Caesar could be revoked by the following one, with the landowner standing to lose his life in the process. It was only prudent in those times to be sure of a place to hide in a case of political turmoil or local uprisings. And that was exactly what the original owner of what was now Foxdale had done—he had built himself an escape route and a hiding place.

Apparently Victor had either known about such things before he'd ever met Vera Solane, or her mother had known that the subterranean chambers and tunnels existed and had mentioned it to him. Had Victor married her just to have access to the estate? Caroline found that hard to believe, given the way he'd spoken of Vera on Sunday night. . . . Yet, it wouldn't be the first time someone lied about his feelings for material gain. It was possible that Victor was nothing more than a deceitful, manipulative con artist. Caroline had to smile at the ironic play on words.

Finding no one downstairs when she got back to Foxdale, Caroline went upstairs to see if her mother was in her suite of rooms. It was later than she'd thought, but Caroline was pleased to note that Victor wasn't home yet. She wanted to talk to her mother alone, without interruption.

"Hello, dear," Vera called out through the open doorway. "Have a nice time?"

Caroline entered the sitting room and looked at her mother tenderly. Vera had just lost her career. How could she now face the tragedy of losing Victor as well? Even if her mother didn't love her husband in a romantic sense, Caroline knew that Vera respected Victor enormously, and that she depended on him emotionally as well as financially.

"Pat was asking for you about an hour or so ago," she said to her daughter. "I told him you'd gone to town, and he seemed surprised. Did you have a date this afternoon?"

"No," Caroline replied. "Maybe he just wanted to talk to me about something."

"So," Vera said, placing the book she'd been reading facedown and smiling expectantly, "tell me what you've been up to while you were in Badalona."

Caroline seated herself in the loveseat across from her mother. "Oh, I was just checking out something. Did you know that Foxdale has secret chambers and tunnels underground?"

"Of course, dear. Your father used to use the tunnel as a wine cellar."

"I never knew about it," Caroline remarked, surprised.

"He didn't want you to. Elliot was worried that you'd either get lost down there, or worse, somehow seal yourself in and not know how to get back out. I never went down there myself...too dirty, filled with cobwebs and Lord knows what else!"

"Do you know how to get into the tunnel?" Caroline asked, her pulse accelerating with anticipation.

"I suppose so. Let's see if I can remember. I think there's a lever inside the bookcase." Vera paused before adding, "I hadn't thought about it until now, but it's funny that Victor should have redecorated that room but not removed the bookcase."

"Where in the bookcase, mother?"

"Umm...if I recall correctly, there's a lever built into one of the bottom shelves. It's too low for eye-level, and one would hardly see it anyway, since it's flush to the shelf and behind the books."

"I'd like to explore it someday," Caroline said, avoiding her mother's eyes.

"And you went all the way to town just to verify that the tunnel existed?" her mother asked, surprised. "Why didn't you ask me first, darling? It's much too hot for you to be trekking around dusty roads!"

Caroline had to laugh. "It never occured to me that you'd know about it," she answered truthfully. "But I seemed to remember the kids at school talking about this house when I was little. They thought it was a wonderful mystery, and I thought it would be fun to check it out." Caroline didn't want to lie, but she couldn't bring herself to reveal what she suspected of Victor—not yet.

Vera smiled pleasantly, obviously losing interest in the conversation. She picked up her book and asked, "Why don't you see if you can find Pat, dear? I'm in the last chapter, and I'd like to finish this before Victor returns."

"What time do you expect him?" Caroline asked.

"He didn't say precisely. Just late afternoon, and it's already past four."

"All right, mother," Caroline said, standing. "I'll see you later then."

Caroline went downstairs and decided to go to her room to freshen up. Turning into the hallway, she almost collided with Victor. "I didn't realize you'd returned," she blurted, a little flustered.

"Just a few moments ago," he said amiably. "I had to put away a few things in my study before going up to see Vera."

"I didn't hear a car," Caroline said, trying not to sound suspicious.

"Probably because you were upstairs, Caroline." He smiled, but his icy blue eyes had no mirth in them. Then, nodding, he moved past her. She could hear his leather shoes on the tile steps as he went up the stairs.

She was disappointed that he'd come back so soon. Now she'd have to wait until the middle of the night to try to find the lever in the bookcase—and to solve the mystery of what Victor was up to. Whatever it was, the answer was underground. And the reason he hadn't needed the car that morning, and she hadn't heard one arriving a few moments ago, was only because he hadn't required one. Victor only had to push a lever and go through the passageway to the underground chamber....

SHE FOUND PAT out in the shed where the old winemaking tools were stored. He was cleaning the old iron winepress, whistling softly to himself. "Hi!" he said when he saw Caroline. "Come on in where it's cool," he called to her, his sleeves rolled up and the muscles in his forearms glistening.

"Have you decided to restore the winery after all?" She took one of the hundreds of baskets used for picking the grapes and turned it upside down for a seat.

"No, but that's no reason for them to let the equipment deteriorate. I thought it would be interesting to restore all of these old tools and have them on exhibit once the winery is operating again. I thought I'd fix up the old forge so I could make the iron hoops that go around the casks, that sort of thing. Once we're in business, I think we could have a nice tourist attraction with some of these artifacts."

She watched him as he worked, noting how content he was to be using his hands and doing something constructive. Pat was the sort of man who'd probably become morose if he couldn't get out of doors and she wondered how he'd ever managed to endure school or rainy days.

"I was looking for you earlier," he said. "Thought you might like to go for a swim or maybe go sailing. Vera said you'd gone into town."

"That's right."

He looked up, scrutinizing her. "Why didn't you ask Alejandro to drive you instead of walking in this heat?"

Caroline hesitated for only a second. "Because I don't trust him," she explained slowly.

"Because he's so ugly?" Pat laughed good-naturedly.

"No, because of last night."

"Want to tell me about it?" Pat continued to scrape at the piece of iron in his hands, not looking at her.

"I think the time is right to tell someone," she answered seriously, adding, "at least a part of it. Pat, I think Alejandro is involved in something highly suspect. I went into town to see if my theory could be verified." Then, with an almost detached air, Caroline told Pat about what she'd observed at the cove before he had arrived on the scene. She was careful to make no mention of Victor or the matter of all the paintings being removed. Pat loved and respected his uncle, and Caroline didn't feel he was ready for the information . . . at least, not until she had some genuine evidence. "And that's why I went to town today," she concluded when she had finished telling her story. "I went to get proof that such a door could exist and find out what it might lead to."

"And did you?" By then Pat's interest had been piqued enough for him to stop working. He was now sitting across from her, leaning against an old cask.

"Yes, there's a map of this estate showing its original construction."

"Whew! I never would have thought that Alejandro might get involved in something illegal," Pat said after a moment. "Victor would throw him out instantly if he knew about it."

"Then you'll appreciate why I didn't tell you before," she said, still skirting Victor's involvement. It was plain to Caroline now that the servant was acting out of devoted loyalty, not deceiving his employer as Pat thought. Victor was the mastermind, and Alejandro was merely his accomplice. But she couldn't prove that, yet.

Pat nodded gravely. "So what do you plan to do now?"

She shrugged. "The obvious. I'm going to go down there and find out what's happening."

"That could be dangerous," Patrick warned, a concerned look in his hazel eyes.

"Not if you help," she replied. "Can you somehow keep Alejandro occupied tonight, especially after everyone else has gone to bed?"

"Meaning?"

"Only that if he's with you, I think I can manage to get into the chamber and see what's there. Once we have some evidence, we can phone the authorities," Caroline explained.

The corners of Pat's sensuous mouth turned down as he thought it over. "Well, he loves to play cribbage. I can keep him busy for hours that way. But I don't like the idea of you going in there all by yourself. What if Alejandro has a partner living down there?"

Caroline shook her head. "It would be too risky for

him," she said, confident that Victor and Alejandro were in their scheme alone. She'd read enough mysteries to know that smart criminals keep their accomplices to a minimum.

"All right," Pat said reluctantly. "But leave the light on in your room. That way it'll seem as if you're staying up late reading. And when I see the light go off, I'll know you're back safely."

"Thank you, Pat. It shouldn't take me too long."

"I can't wait to hear about what you find," he said, grinning conspiratorially. "It'll hurt Victor to learn that his trusted servant isn't what he thought, but he'll do what he must."

"Yes, I'm sure of it," she replied, wondering just how far Victor would go when he was cornered.

Chapter 16

She waited a full hour after everyone had retired for the night, pacing her room impatiently. Caroline had deliberately worn a very feminine summer dress at dinner and had gone out of her way to be affable and congenial during the meal. She spoke of how well John had liked Victor and Vera, how much he'd enjoyed his brief visit, and she deliberately complimented Victor on some of the new paintings he'd put up.

"Yes, they'll be famous one day. Like fine wines," Victor had said. "It's often better to buy them while they're still very young—it costs infinitely less, and your investment can only mature."

When they were saying good-night, Victor had put his arm around Caroline's shoulder and kissed her gently on the cheek for the first time. He'd been warm and outgoing, obviously enjoying himself immensely.

Vera also had displayed a return to her former good spirits, clearly pleased that her daughter and husband were getting on so well. Though Pat had remained in the background for the evening, he had been congenial company, adding agreeably, if only occasionally, to the dinnertime conversation.

It had all gone splendidly well, but now it was time to find the lever in the bookshelves. She had already smuggled a flashlight into her room, and had changed into suitable clothes for her foray into the tunnel. Glancing at her travel clock, she saw that it was after one o'clock. Everyone should be asleep, she thought, and prepared to leave her room.

The stillness of the house unnerved her as she crept down the hall and opened the door to Victor's study. Once inside, she turned on the flashlight and dropped to her knees in front of the bookcase. Cautiously, she began to pull the books out, starting with the bottom shelf.

She found the lever behind the third book, a thick volume on the history of Spain in the middle ages. Up until then, she had been methodical and in complete control of herself. But seeing the lever, her excitement began to mount.

Carefully, she pushed it from left to right and stood back expectantly. Slowly, the entire case began to move away from the wall toward her. It didn't open wide, just enough for a broad-shouldered man to walk through. But that was enough for Victor's purposes, paintings were narrow regardless of how long or wide they were.

Caroline flashed the light into the opening and saw beams supporting the dirt walls and ceiling of the tunnel. She stepped inside, looking for a way to close the bookcase again, then decided it didn't matter. Victor was upstairs with her mother, and Patrick was keeping Alejandro occupied.

Cautiously, Caroline began to walk down the incline in the tunnel. She could smell the dank earth around her and couldn't stop herself from comparing the tunnel to a tomb. As she proceeded through the tunnel, she began to hear a strange kind of humming, almost like an air conditioner but quieter. She stopped to listen, and the dirt beneath her feet vibrated slightly. Whatever had caused the trembling of the ground near the rose garden must have originated down here, she thought. She waited for a few seconds. and then the sound and motion stopped abruptly.

She progressed slowly, almost inching her way along, her tension increasing with each passing minute. The chamber couldn't be far now, she realized, remembering the drawing in the museum.

Thick wooden planks served as stairs as the way became suddenly steeper. The flashlight revealed ancient torches affixed to the sides of the beams in this section, and Caroline was sure that their fires would only have intensified the eerie quality of the tunnel. How many people had stolen through this passageway, she wondered. It was close to two thousand years old.... What secrets could the walls reveal?

Just beyond the bottom step, about four yards ahead, she could make out a heavy plank door with a crude latch. Light was visible under the door. This had to be the chamber, but how could she tell if anyone was inside it?

Frightened, but determined, she walked slowly to the door and put her hand on the latch. With her pulse pounding in her ears, she simultaneously turned off the flashlight and opened the heavy door.

She was momentarily blinded by the brightness within, then her eyes began to adjust. Caroline could scarcely believe what she saw. Not even the most sumptuous London galleries were as meticulously planned as this chamber. It was constructed like a maze, with perfectly illuminated paintings everywhere she looked. Stepping inside slowly, her eyes fell on the Cézanne that had been in the living room. Near it was a Mondrian, and just beyond, an Orozco and a Rousseau.

It was like a fantasy world for art lovers. Everything had been arranged to best display the paintings, and Caroline was nearly mesmerized by the planner's perfection.

"I've been waiting for you, my dear."

Though she recognized Victor's voice, she was still too stunned to react immediately.

"Would you like a tour, as long as you're here? You'll never see such a collection in one place again—not as long as you live."

"How did you know I'd found out?" she finally asked, her eyes wide as he came toward her. He was holding a glass of sherry and smiling at her cordially like a host at a private party. There was nothing in the least intimidating about Victor; he seemed perfectly relaxed.

Taking her by the elbow, he led her into the room. "Some of these works you may not have learned about in school, but they are masterpieces nevertheless. This one, for instance," he said, pausing. "Are you familiar with the work of Hodler? He was Viennese, and one of the major painters of the Vienna Secession movement. Intriguing, isn't it?"

Caroline could barely nod as they moved on through the corridors of art. As they turned one corner, a salon came into view, and Victor led her to a comfortable armchair. "You still haven't told me how you knew..." Caroline asked.

"It was only a matter of time," he said airily. "First you said you were an art student, and then you noticed vibrations from the equipment I have down here to control the temperature and humidity.... I knew there was little I could do to keep the truth from you. I knew my story about rotating the paintings wouldn't fool you for long," he concluded.

"You give me too much credit, Victor," she answered levelly as he poured a sherry for her. "Even when you removed the paintings, I still wasn't really alerted to something being wrong."

"What finally tipped the balance?" he asked with casual interest, almost as if they were discussing the weather.

Caroline then told him about the dinghy and seeing Alejandro walking out of the wall of the cliff. Finally she explained how she had gone to Barcelona that afternoon to find out about the original construction of the buildings.

Victor nodded when she'd finished speaking as if nothing she'd said surprised him in the least. "The old paintings were my main reason for wanting to restore this estate," he explained. "I wanted to live here quietly with your beautiful mother while I feasted my eyes and my soul on these beautiful works of art."

"Did you marry mother to get this house?" Caroline asked softly.

He smiled patiently. "No, I married her because I adored her. This house was merely a bonus. Of course, as your mother's husband, I knew I'd have some say over what was done to the estate and would certainly be able to veto any notion she might have to sell it."

"Then you did love her?"

Nodding, Victor replied, "I did, and I do. However, it was a small shock when I learned yesterday that she'd already turned Foxdale over to you. You realize, of course, that Vera has no idea of what I've created down here."

"Yes, I know," she answered. "But you still haven't told me how you knew I was coming here tonight." Oddly enough, Caroline felt completely calm, as if there was nothing unusual at all about this nocturnal conversation. Victor was just as pleasant now as he'd been during dinner and afterward.

He shrugged, a slight smile curling his lips. "Pat hasn't played cribbage with Alejandro since the lad was sixteen. This sudden renewal of their acquaintance, especially with a lovely young woman in the house, seemed a bit curious."

Caroline was mildly amused at how easily their plot had been uncovered. "May I ask you something else?"

"Of course, my dear," Victor replied. "You and I have no secrets anymore, have we?"

Her admiration for his smooth detached manner was increasing by the second. "How did you manage to amass this collection without a single theft being reported?"

Victor took a sip of his sherry, a bemused expression on his face. "It was terribly easy and almost childishly simple," he said. "As a dealer for so many years, I came to know the best art forgers—their names, at least, and where they live, if they're not in prison. I hired several over the years to copy the paintings I wanted. Then, when the time was right, I arranged for the original and the forgery to be exchanged. Since no one was ever caught for breaking in, and nothing looked different to the guards, the gallery people never knew a theft had occurred."

"But surely one day . . . ."

He waved his thin hand. "Perhaps, but I doubt it. They were master forgeries, and I was serious when I said that people tend to take for granted what they see in the same place every day. Only an art expert could detect my forgeries, and even so, it would take more than a cursory examination. If a painting isn't missing, why would it occur to anyone that a substitution—indeed anything extraordinary—had taken place?"

Caroline had to smile at the simplicity of his plan. Unless one of his men was actually caught in the act of stealing from one of the museums or galleries, no one would ever be the wiser. "Then, you're not selling the paintings?" she asked.

"Sell them! My dear girl, never! They're mine now, as precious to me as life itself. I would never risk them falling into the hands of someone who didn't appreciate them. They're loved here, looked after—every stroke of the brush is exquisitely appreciated!"

"My God!"

At the sound of Patrick's voice both Victor and Caroline turned at the same time. She felt sorry for Pat as he stood in the doorway, his eyes huge as he took in the chamber. "It's all right, Patrick," she said soothingly. "Come in."

He came forward with unsure steps, disbelief and awe on his face. "What is this?" he asked.

Victor laughed lightly. "My world, Pat. My nirvana."

"Except now you'll have to give them back, Victor," Caroline said quietly, gesturing to the paintings.

"I suppose so," he admitted softly. "And the police will come. . . . I'll be arrested, of course."

"You don't seem to mind," she remarked.

Patrick stood a little apart, looking as if he'd walked into Alice's looking glass. "They're all stolen?" he asked in a whisper.

"Of course, my boy," Victor answered easily. "And Caroline cleverly figured it out."

"But you said you thought Alejandro was a crook, Caroline. You made no mention of Victor!" Pat said indignantly.

"If I had, would you have believed me?" Without waiting for a reply, she turned back to Victor. "It shouldn't be a very long sentence, Victor. You're not guilty of violence or causing anyone harm."

"Yes, I know. I checked into the laws before I began my private campaign to save these works of art. Most museums aren't safe places for paintings anymore, you know. Smog, exhaust fumes—it all gets inside and eats at the pigment."

"Do you want to tell mother, or shall I?" asked Caroline.

"No, it's up to me to break it to her." Victor replied.

"I'd appreciate it, though, if you would stay on to be with her while I'm gone."

Caroline smiled ruefully, knowing now why he'd made up the little story about her mother wanting her to stay. When she didn't answer at once, Victor sighed and got to his feet.

"Well, shall we go back up now?" he asked almost cheerfully. "We'll all need a good night's rest before facing tomorrow."

AFTER THE POLICE HAD LEFT, Vera, Patrick and Caroline sat quietly in the living room, all three wrapped in their own thoughts. Soon the art experts would begin to arrive, and the chamber would be emptied gradually as the experts reclaimed the masterpieces they had never known were gone.

"He's a hero in his own way, you know," Vera said finally. "He thought he could preserve them for a while. But maybe it wasn't all in vain. At least now, the publicity may spur the curators to seal the windows and take better care of the paintings."

Caroline glanced over at her mother, who was dressed completely in black, as if in mourning. She was taking Victor's imprisonment better than Caroline had anticipated. Vera was being "noble," and the role suited her quite well.

"I think I'll go and lie down for a while," she said, her deep voice miraculously managing to sound fragile.

Pat rose to his feet as Vera stood up. She patted his arm gently, appreciatively, and with a wistful smile, left the room.

"Have you decided what you're going to do?" Patrick

said, coming over and sitting down on the sofa next to Caroline.

"I'll go home next week," she said, pausing as she formulated her thoughts.

"Even if I tell you that I'm in love with you?"

She looked into his eyes and saw the steady sincerity in them, then smiled.

"Are you laughing at me, then?" Patrick's brogue was back and his hazel eyes had become troubled.

"You didn't let me finish," she explained. "I'll go back to England and tell the Clarkes what's happened. I'll have to let Johnnie down as gently as I can, and that will take a little time. Then I'll arrange for my transfer to the University of Barcelona."

Patrick's face became suffused with pleasure. "Then there's a chance for me in your life?"

"You have to answer two questions first," she teased.

"Anything!"

"Why did you follow me into the tunnel?"

He grinned smugly. "You turned your light out, Caroline! You were supposed to leave it on, remember? I thought something was wrong, so came in search of you, ready to do battle with a gang of pirates to save you!"

Caroline put her hand into his, her brown eyes sparkling with happiness. "Next question...why do you intend to blend the *Rioja* wines? Couldn't you leave them pure?"

Patrick's laugh filled the room as he put his arm around her shoulder. "You had to wait until now to ask?" he said, sounding incredulous.

"I was afraid of your answer," she said adding, "and I knew it was none of my business."

He nodded, pretending to assimilate this information very seriously. "My dear Caroline, the blended wine will not be for the connoisseurs."

"Then . . . ?"

"The blended wine will have a limited bottling, only for export to the damned English, who can't tell the difference anyhow!"

"Oh Patrick! I'm so relieved!"

"And where's my reward for this brilliant solution?" he asked as his lips closed over hers and her arms reached up to hold him tightly.

It would only be a brief separation. . . . She'd soon be back and in his embrace forever.

4 FREE

MYSTIQUE BOOKS
Your FREE gift includes . . .

Exciting novels of romance, suspense and drama, with intriguing characters and surprising plot twists, set against international backgrounds.

PROPER AGE FOR LOVE, *Claudette Jaunière*
Anne didn't understand when her fiancé suggested she become his mistress — not his wife. And so she fled across Europe into a nightmare of intrigue and danger where her very survival depended on the man she most loved — and feared.

ISLAND OF DECEIT, *Alix André*
Determined to discover her sister's fate on an exotic Caribbean isle, Rosalie finds herself enmeshed in a web of lies, dangerously attracted to the only man who might know the dreadful truth.

HIGH WIND IN BRITTANY, *Caroline Gayet*
What elaborate charade of identity was the stranger playing on the tiny coastal town? Only Marie knew, and her knowledge brought her danger.

HOUSE OF SECRETS, *Denise Noël*
Would Pascale reveal a family secret kept hidden for years . . . or stand accused of murdering another woman to protect the man she loved?

Your FREE gift includes

House of Secrets—by Denise Noël
Proper Age for Love—by Claudette Jaunière
Island of Deceit—by Alix André
High Wind in Brittany—by Caroline Gayet

Mail this coupon today!

FREE GIFT CERTIFICATE
and Subscription Reservation

Mail this coupon today.
To: Mystique Books

In U.S.A.
M.P.O. Box 707
Niagara Falls, NY 14302

In Canada
649 Ontario Street
Stratford, Ontario, M5A 6W2

Please send me my 4 Mystique Books **free.**
Also, reserve a subscription to the 4 NEW
Mystique Books published each month. Each
month I will receive 4 NEW Mystique Books at
the low price of $1.50 [total $6.00 a month].

There are no shipping and handling nor any
other hidden charges. I may cancel this
arrangement at any time, but even if I do, these
first 4 books are still mine to keep.

My present
membership
number is

NAME   (PLEASE PRINT)

ADDRESS

CITY   STATE/PROV.   ZIP/POSTAL CODE

Offer not valid for present Mystique subscribers.
Offer expires August 31, 1980.
Prices subject to change without notice.

00256456200